CU00867350

Julia

The Teenage Years

Book 4

MAYHEM

Katrina Kahler

Copyright © KC Global Enterprises Pty Ltd

Table of Contents

If only…

My mind spun with crazed images that raced around and around relentlessly inside my head. The overwhelming panic was so intense that I found it difficult to breathe. Gasping for air, I clutched at the chair in front of me, fearful that I would collapse right there, right then. But perhaps that would not be such a bad thing. Surely, any escape from the guilt that I was immersed in could only be welcomed.

Aware that it was entirely my fault, made it so much harder to bear.

I was to blame.

Me.

I had caused this. And now there was nothing I could do except pray.

Desperately, I wanted to run away…escape to another world where disaster ceased to exist.

Why, oh why?

If only I could rewind the series of events. Take them all back and press 'Play' once more; create a new reality, one very different to the confusion and despair that had come to pass.

If only.

Twelve hours earlier…

The days had flown by in a blur. I was in state of pure bliss and nothing could shake the happiness that engulfed me. At times, I stopped to reflect on the past few weeks, and had to remind myself that the dream I was living, actually was my reality. For the first time in as long as I could remember, I felt safe, secure and truly happy.

The sight of Ky's beautiful face was what came to mind the very second I opened my eyes each morning, and thoughts of him were my last, before finally drifting off to sleep at night. It was like a blissful, never ending dream and I marveled at how my life seemed to have done a complete turn-around ever since he'd become such a close part of it.

As I rolled over in bed, and stared through the open window to the darkened sky beyond, I pictured once more in my mind, the wonderful smile that never ceased to cause the delightful sparks that it always did whenever I saw him. Just that day, Becky had asked me in her usual inquisitive manner, what it was that I liked most about Ky. And my answer had been simple. Without any hesitation whatsoever, I replied, knowing instantly what it was that I treasured most.

His smile. That beautiful, gorgeous, cheeky wonderful grin of his, which, from the moment he saw me each morning at school, instantly lit his stunning features. And each and every time, without fail, the butterflies in my stomach would dance their little dance and the familiar jolts of electric pleasure would pass between us.

Those thoughts alone were enough to cause a wild grin to

form on my own face and the thrill that I felt at the very thought of his sweet lips on mine when he kissed me goodbye that very afternoon, threw me into such a frenzy that I thought I would never be able to fall asleep.

Rolling over once more, an image of Millie's face abruptly came to mind and I was reminded of the Facebook message I'd received a short time earlier, telling me that she'd arrived home just that evening and was keen to hang out over the weekend.

It had been about three years since I'd seen the girl who I had once called my best friend. I knew I should be thrilled that I was the first person she wanted to visit after her long holiday abroad. But although terribly excited, I was also nervous and unsure.

Would things be the same between us? Would we still get on the way that we used to? Would she still like me?

I didn't really think I had changed very much, but what about her? And my biggest fear…what would she think of Ky?

Details...

Looking back on the events of that fateful day, I am reminded of how happy I was when I woke that morning; the early morning sunshine streaming through my opened curtains and falling delicately across my face. I loved to wake up that way, the warmth of the sun creating an inner glow inside me, as its rays skipped across my bedroom and rested gently on my bed. Summer was fast approaching and I was overcome with anticipation over what it would bring. I could barely wait for school to be over. Ky and I had so many plans and I knew it would be a summer to remember.

That morning however, there was another reason for the instant smile that had formed on my face as soon as I recalled my plans. I'd been waiting for so long and finally the day had arrived. Although the thought of seeing my best friend again had created an inner anxiety the evening before, which was something I had not expected, I'd decided to cast all silly thoughts aside and simply focus on the joy of seeing Millie again. And that was all it had taken. The anxiety had disappeared, and in its place stood nervous excitement.

Right then, I felt more eager than ever. And this was due to what I called my brain-wave, which had occurred just the night before.

I know, what I can do! Get Millie a welcome home gift.

The thought had entered my mind out of the blue as I sat staring at the photo I kept of her, mounted in a rectangular silver frame on the bookcase that stood along the wall near my bed. It was such an old photo, one that had been taken several years earlier, but that single shot captured our friendship completely.

I had my arm draped loosely around Millie's shoulder, as we sat side by side on the top step at the front of my house. My mom had snapped the pic when we weren't looking, but the image was a clear indication of the close friendship we had once shared, and I definitely considered it my most favorite of all the photos taken of us together. Millie's sparkling eyes were crinkled at the corners and her face tilted slightly upwards, her mouth open wide with laughter. I looked happily towards her, my own wide smile also capturing the special moment. It was one of so many distinctive memories, but that particular photo captured the image beautifully.

I knew exactly what type of photo frame I would buy as a gift for my friend. I had in mind the double sided style, where on one side, I could insert a copy of my favorite pic, and the other side I would leave blank, ready to insert the selfie that I planned to take that very afternoon. Visualizing in my mind, the two of us mimicking that exact same pose, I draped my arm around Millie's shoulder, while the two of us sat enjoying each other's company once more.

"It's going to be just like the old days!" Millie had said in her message the evening before, and I was convinced that my idea was the perfect welcome home present.

There was one small niggling doubt however, that still played mercilessly at the rear of my mind. Although I'd tried to shake it, it had remained in place and was continuing to bother me.

Ky was in my life now, and our relationship was much more than an innocent childhood crush. It was not simply a middle school romance that involved hanging out at school and on the occasional weekend. It was much, much more than that and I just hoped Millie would understand.

Surely though, there was room in my life for both of them; a best friend and the boy of my dreams, the one who I had fallen deeply and helplessly in love with.

Sighing heavily, I tried again to erase the worry that lingered within my thoughts. Why I was feeling such a sensation of dread was beyond me.

I had previously learned to listen to my intuition, but that morning I was way too preoccupied, and stood quickly, after remembering that I needed to claim the bathroom before my brother. If I waited any longer, he would be sure to get there first and then I'd never have time for all that I'd planned.

Ky, being the wonderful person that he was, had agreed to meet me at the local shopping center to help choose the perfect photo frame. He was happy to help with my choice and it made me so happy to see him excited to meet Millie, the friend I had spoken so much about during the past weeks.

At first he'd offered to pick me up so that we could go to the shops together but then, when his grandmother asked him to run some errands for her, our plans changed. That was when I decided to simply meet him there and take advantage of some time on my own to browse the shopping center to look for a present for his birthday.

It was fast approaching and I was at a loss for what I could give him. Some alone time at the shops was a perfect opportunity to search for the ideal gift.

My main problem in that department though, was having enough money with which to buy it. Although our dad gave my brother, Matt and I a weekly allowance, it was only a small amount, and I knew that I desperately needed to get myself a part-time job. That was definitely on my to-do list for the summer break, and I was aware that I needed to start applying soon, before all the positions were taken.

So many details and so much trivia had filled my mind that morning. But the one niggling thought that had any real significance was the one I'd chosen to ignore. Hindsight is a wonderful thing, and looking back now, I am still conscious of the gut feeling that had tried to take hold. I'm sure it had been a warning, but too caught up in the events ahead, I'd pushed it completely away.

And then, only a short time later, it was too late.

The passing of time...

Just parked the car. Heading over now xx

As soon as I received his text, I raced from the shops where I was idly browsing for his present. I had found a few perfect options and was thrilled that I may have actually solved the problem of finding an ideal present; one that I knew he would love. And then I heard the familiar sound from my phone alerting me to his message.

Racing towards our pre-arranged meeting place which was in a different shopping complex across the road, I was held up by the parents of a friend from school and I was forced to stop and chat in order to be polite. But after a very quick conversation, I excused myself and made my way hurriedly through the center, in the hope that I hadn't kept him waiting.

When I reached the exit, I spotted him amongst the pedestrians crossing to the other side of the street. All I caught was a glimpse, but I recognized him immediately. His tall muscular physique and the toss of his tousled and sun streaked hair as he made his way across the road, was instantly recognizable. And just the mere sight of him caused my skin to tingle. I could feel the smile erupt on my face, the delight at knowing he was on his way to meet me, rapidly filling me with joy.

"Ky!" I called excitedly, as soon as I glimpsed his familiar figure.

"Ky!" I repeated once more.

At the sound of his name being called, he stopped for a

moment and looked around, the surrounding crowd continuing on their way. It was probably only a second or two, but that was all it had taken for the roadway to be cleared. Cleared of everyone that was, except Ky.

Turning back towards the sound of my voice, he paused momentarily, taking time to wave in recognition. And instantly, that wonderful, beautiful, mesmerizing smile of his had appeared.

Only to be whisked quickly away.

It was like the scene of a movie unraveling before my very eyes, except that for some strange reason, it appeared to be happening in slow motion. Almost as though I were viewing it one frame at a time.

Tick, tock, tick, tock. Time passed by the way it usually does, but at that one crucial moment, when it all took place, time appeared to slip by ever so slowly. And as I stood on the edge of the sidewalk watching the scene in front of me unfold, it seemed as though that mysterious concept called time, decided to abruptly stand still.

The car that hit him had come from nowhere. Almost out of thin air, it had appeared. And then it was gone. The only evidence of an accident was Ky's body lying lifeless on the ground.

That's how it happened. And it was all my fault.

That very scene flashed vividly through my thoughts. Over and over and over.

And I was convinced it would be etched on my mind forever.

Fear...

I held his hand all the way to the hospital.

"Please Ky!" I sobbed. "Please be okay!"

The paramedics in the ambulance tried to console me.

"He's still breathing," the lady said. "Just hold his hand and let him know you're here."

"No, no, no, no," the words inside me screamed. "This can't be happening!"

But it *was* happening and I was left waiting. Waiting to hear some news. Any news. And desperately hoping that he would be okay.

As I paced the hospital waiting room, I dreaded the sight of his grandmother appearing before me, knowing full well that she would surely not be far away. The nurse had finally managed to track her down and I could only imagine her absolute horror at the news of Ky's accident, as soon as she heard.

How could I face her? How could I admit that I was to blame?

If only I hadn't called out to him. If only I hadn't insisted that he meet me. If only I had simply gone shopping on my own.

Sick with dread, I waited anxiously for her arrival, expecting her to be there at any moment.

As I continued to pace, I looked frantically around for a

doctor, a nurse, anyone who could tell me what was going on.

"As soon as we know how he is, we will tell you." The nurse had attempted to reassure me with soothing words, as she ushered me into the waiting room, giving me strict instructions to stay there. But an hour later, still with no news, I was on the verge of hysteria.

Blame...

When I saw her face, I was overwhelmed with pity. That beautiful old lady. She had so much to worry about already, with a young grandson suffering autism and now she was lumbered with this.

Why was life so unfair? Why did some people have to deal with so much while others seemed to breeze through their existence? It just wasn't right.

"Mrs. Roberston!" I called, as soon as I saw her heading in my direction.

Standing up from the seat where I'd been waiting alone, I raced towards her and it was then that the tears I'd been holding back, burst quickly forth.

Like a dam that had abruptly broken its banks, my sadness and despair flowed freely onto her shoulder as she hugged me tightly.

"He's in a coma!" I sobbed, barely able to speak the words that she needed to hear. "Oh, Mrs. Roberston. It's all my fault!"

She faltered then, and took a step back, shaking her head in confusion. I could see that she had not comprehended a word.

"What do you mean, Julia? And where is he? I want to see him."

Brushing me aside, she made her way quickly towards the nurses' station, demanding to see Ky and to be informed of the details.

"Where's his doctor?" she asked sharply. "Please can you find him? I want to know what's going on. Please hurry. I need to see the doctor. And I need to see my grandson!"

A look of understanding appeared on the nurse's face as she led Ky's grandmother towards the room where he lay. But all I could do was stand by and watch.

As I stared at her forlorn figure heading down the hallway towards his room, I heard the distinctive blip of a Facebook message alerting me to my phone. At first I was tempted to ignore it. I did not want to speak to anyone, not even by text or messenger. All I wanted was to run away, escape to another place, where Ky and I could begin our day again. Start over so that I could see his beautiful smile once more and feel the touch of his hand in mine.

But instead, all I was faced with was the sight of doctors and nurses and the love of my life laying deathly still in a hospital bed. The tubes and life support machines stood like ugly sentinels on guard at his side; an instant reminder of the tragic accident just a short time earlier.

The persistent blip of my phone forced me to pull it from my pocket, anything to stop that irritating sound. I would turn it off if need be. I just wanted to be left alone.

A quick glance at the screen highlighted Millie's name.

Millie. The reason for the continuous messages right then and also the reason why Ky and I both happened to be at the shopping center in the first place.

Deep down, I was fully aware she had nothing to do with what had happened. She was just an innocent piece of the puzzle that had so wrongly been put together. But I could not help my feelings. I was overcome with sorrow and guilt and despair. And I needed someone to blame.

Ignoring her message completely, I shoved the phone roughly back into my pocket.

Millie was the last person I wanted to speak to.

Ky needed me. And nothing else mattered.

Guilt...

As I sat by his bedside later that evening, I felt drained beyond comprehension. I'd cried so much already that I seemed to have no tears left to cry. And, turning down all offers of food from the nurses who kept appearing in order to monitor the various machines, I also rejected all suggestions to go home and rest. I was adamant that I would not leave, not until he woke up and I knew that he was okay. Until that moment, I vowed that I would remain right there and that nobody was going to make me do otherwise.

His grandmother had left a short time earlier. She had another grandson who also needed care, and I'd promised to call her immediately if there was any change in his condition.

With my head resting on the back of the padded chair that sat in the corner of the room, I closed my eyes for a moment; but instantly, the memory of that morning appeared. Vivid and abrupt, the scenes played out one at a time as I recalled every second that led to the sight of his body laying lifeless on the road in front of me.

And then, my thoughts abruptly switched to the scene I had interrupted just an hour ago, when I returned from the bathroom to discover two police officers, deep in conversation with Mrs. Robertson. I had caught them mid-sentence and stood quietly at the doorway to listen in on what they were saying.

"It was a hit and run," one of the policemen explained, the compassion clear in his voice. "But a quick thinking eye-witness took a photo of the driver's number plate and we were able to locate him a short time later."

"After some investigation, we managed to determine that he'd been texting on his phone, and had driven straight through a red light. When he realized he'd hit someone, instead of stopping he just kept driving."

With nausea churning in the pit of my stomach and threatening to explode, I stared speechless at the officer. He then turned abruptly in my direction, the sound of the audible gasp that had escaped my lips, catching his attention.

Glancing towards Ky and then to his grandmother, I could see that she too was overcome, her face white with shock as she sat beside his bed, her mouth open wide in horror and grief.

"The driver is a 19 year old male, who apparently was texting his girlfriend at the time, to tell her he was going to be late," the other policeman continued, the disgust in his tone so noticeable, I could almost feel it.

"He's now in custody and will definitely be facing a jail sentence. It's an absolute disgrace that accidents like this happen because irresponsible drivers are using mobile phones. And to be texting while driving is sheer stupidity!"

Recalling their words only caused my stomach to churn once again, the bile rising to my throat as I pictured that driver, his identity unknown to me and his face a blank. In my mind's eye, I could see the phone in his hand while he sped through the intersection and ran down the innocent person who just happened to be on the crossing at that very moment.

But that innocent person was not some random pedestrian, one who I later pitied and felt sorry for, after hearing the evening news. By some bizarre quirk of fate, it was Ky who'd been hit and left lifeless on the road, as if simply a piece of discarded rubbish, overlooked and unwanted.

The police officers' compassionate expressions and sympathetic words only added to the feeling of despair that suffocated the room as we sat by Ky's bedside, too overcome with emotion to speak. And then they had left, unwilling or unable to stay any longer.

That was when my gaze fell once more upon Ky's beautiful face, and I was forced to voice the thought that had been at the forefront of my mind from the beginning. "It's my fault. If I hadn't distracted him, he would have already crossed safely to the other side of the road, and he wouldn't be laying here now!"

Regardless of what the police had said, I could not overcome the guilt I was feeling and I stared in desperation at his grandmother.

"Julia, you heard the officers." She was adamant in her response, her tone firm and unwavering.

"You can't blame yourself for this! The driver is the guilty one, not you. And what we must focus on right now, is a full recovery. Ky needs you to be strong, Julia. Be strong for him and I'm sure he'll come back to us."

Although I could clearly see the logic and sense in her words, it contradicted so intensely with my guilt, and I was convinced that remorse would always maintain a prime position in the recesses of my mind.

But I looked at her then, the authority in her voice and the words she was saying making their way slowly through to my subconscious, the place where all my hidden thoughts and deepest regrets lay. And I could feel the battle there, taking place while I stared back at her in an attempt to believe that what she'd said was true...it wasn't my fault.

And with a determined sigh, I forced a switch in my brain, which in turn forced her message to finally hit home. Ky's recovery was what mattered, not my feelings of self-pity or guilt. As she had said, I needed to focus my strength on his recovery. That was all that counted.

But regardless of my thoughts and emotions or any level of determination on my part, his recovery was something the doctors said only time would tell. Time and prayers and hope and faith. And as I sat there, the minutes ticking by and the beeping sound of the machines attached to his body keeping a regular hypnotic rhythm, I prayed. From the depths of my soul, I begged God to bring Ky back to us.

With tears streaming from my eyes once more, I reached for his hand and whispered to the boy I loved.

"Please Ky. Please get better."

Unexpected...

The next morning, there was still no change. I'd awoken stiff and sore, after eventually falling asleep in the armchair in the corner of the room. And everything appeared exactly as it was the evening before. The machines continued to beep, the nurses continued to monitor the screens and the doctors continued to check on Ky's condition. But it was all to no avail. He remained in a coma and we were still at the mercy of time.

"It's a waiting game," the doctor had said, on his last visit. "All we can do is wait and see." And then he had left the room.

Sighing deeply, I focused on Ky once again. Overwhelmed by frustration and concern I sat holding his hand, at a loss for what to do. My brother had visited the night before, worried about me and anxious about Ky. But I was so glad to have his support. I'd received several text messages from him during the night as well, asking for updates and if there was anything he could do. While I was extremely grateful, the one thing I so desperately wanted and needed, he had no control over. That was all up to Ky.

When Mrs. Robertson arrived later that morning, after leaving Ky's brother, Tyler once more in the care of a neighbor, I could see that she had also slept very little. The concern was etched on her face and her eyes were clouded with worry as she stared at her grandson, laying so still in the bed beside her.

After exchanging a few words, I decided to take advantage of her arrival and excuse myself so that I could use the bathroom and get some much needed fresh air. I desperately wanted to clear my head and walked quickly towards the elevator that led to the floor below and the exit doors for the outside world.

Heading slowly towards the foyer, I held my head down, deep in thought. The next day was a school day but how on earth was I going to go back to my normal life?

It did not seem possible. I did not know how I could ever manage to do that. It was beyond comprehension and I shook my head, unable to come to terms with the idea. My world could not go on as before, not while he remained in hospital, comatose and lifeless. To even contemplate such a thought seemed too cruel.

As the thoughts swirled around and around in my mind, I looked up momentarily; the sound of the electric doors ahead opening wide, and the loud traffic noise from the street beyond, assaulting the quiet space around me. The sound had caught my attention, and I took a quick glance before looking back down at the floor once more. But the vision I'd been confronted with, caused an abrupt double take and I stared in disbelief at the sight of the familiar figure walking towards me.

Although somewhat changed in appearance, with flowing long hair that framed her beautiful face and highlighted the healthy glow of her suntanned skin, her eyes and facial features were still the same. And I knew in a heartbeat that I would recognize that girl anywhere.

Focus...

"Julia!"

The word sprang from her lips and she rushed towards me; her arms opened wide in a welcome embrace as she wrapped them tightly around my shoulders, the affection and warmth as genuine as ever before.

The realization that Millie was there, right by my side when I needed her most, created a feeling so intense that I was unable to prevent the flood of tears that poured out in an unstoppable flow. Tears of sorrow and loss and joy and intense relief combined together and I became a sobbing mess as I stood embracing my long lost friend in the foyer of the hospital in full view of everyone.

Apparently she had turned up at my house earlier that morning, after being unable to contact me the day before. It was then that she'd been confronted with Matt's recount of what had happened and when I still didn't respond to her texts or calls, she decided to go to the hospital and find me.

Then several hours later, she'd been the one to convince me to go home; home to the sanctuary of my bedroom and the comfort of my own bed where I could get the sleep that I so desperately needed.

"The nurses will let you know if there's any change," she had insisted when at first, I shook my head in refusal at her suggestion.

"You'll be no good to Ky if you get sick, yourself. And that's what will happen if you don't go home and get a good night's rest!"

It was those words that finally persuaded me and later that evening, before finally drifting into a deep and soundless sleep, thoughts of Millie's unexpected arrival and the hours that followed, filled me with intense relief once more.

It was so good to have her back. To have the best friend who I once knew and could always rely on, back in my life right when I needed her most. It seemed a miracle of unbelievable proportions. Although her hair was now much longer than ever before, and she had also changed the color to a darker shade, she was still the Millie I had always known. And I was so grateful!

Together we'd taken a walk through a nearby park, the fresh air and distraction was exactly what I needed. And after texting Ky's grandmother, to let her know where I was, Millie and I spent the next two hours sitting in a booth at the back of the hospital café where we talked the entire time.

Although there was so much other news to catch up on, Millie was only interested in hearing about Ky and asked me to share all the details…right from the day that I first noticed him at school. We laughed over the many embarrassing moments I'd experienced throughout my ongoing obsession with him. Right from the start, I'd thought of him as the most divine creature I'd ever laid eyes on, and in a tumble of excitement at the memory, I explained that since meeting him, I'd barely been able to concentrate on anything else.

She insisted on all the details, right up until our very first kiss, all the while commenting on how romantic the story was. But thoughts of his lips on mine brought me tumbling quickly back to the present moment and the reality that now existed; the vision of his crumpled body on the road, where only seconds earlier, he had stood smiling happily towards me, clear in my mind once more.

The feelings of guilt proceeded to take a firm hold yet again and I was powerless to shake them. Opening up to Millie was so easy though. She was the one friend I'd always been able to confide in, and she listened carefully as I bared my soul. In detail, I described my intense remorse over the accident that I still blamed myself for. And when I imagined Ky's beautiful eyes looking into my own, with the warm touch of his hand as he held me close, I prayed for the umpteenth time that he would fully recover.

Rather than dwelling on the accident as I had expected however, along with words of sympathy, the ones that deep down I was still craving, Millie's response was of a completely different nature; a recollection from our past that forced me to sit up and take notice.

"You get what you focus on, Julia! Isn't that what you always used to say to me?"

I looked at her then, silent and unsure. What was she referring to? And what was she implying? Feeling instantly defensive, my response was more abrupt than I intended.

"What do you mean, Millie? Are you saying that I *did* cause the accident?"

"No, Julia," she relied gently. "Of course not! There's no way that you're to blame for what happened. But you can have a big impact on what comes next! I remember you always repeating that phrase to me... 'You get what you focus on!' I used to get sick of hearing it. Surely you remember how powerful those words are!"

Instantly aware of what she was referring to, the memories flashed by in a torrent of waves, rolling through my mind, one after another. There had been so many incidences back in middle school, where everything seemed to go wrong. But I had managed to change my outlook, and before long, circumstances seemed to miraculously improve. At the time, the words she was now reminding me of had been my own mantra. *My Mantra!* The one that I had preached to her on a regular basis.

But what had happened to that wonderful optimistic mindset that I used to possess and was always encouraging in others? Apart from Ky becoming such an amazing part of my life, all I'd experienced since moving back to Carindale was a barrage of drama and problems. Was I to blame for those? Had my state of mind caused the chain of negative events, all the sadness, all the heartache and all the worry?

Perhaps Millie was right. Perhaps it was all due to my constant negativity, forever focusing on doom and gloom and that had simply attracted more and more of the same horrible stuff into my life. It was an epiphany of sorts, and it all seemed to make sense.

The questions whirled through my mind and I looked gratefully towards her. In that instant, I realized more than ever, how glad I was to have her back. Then, taking a deep breath, I spoke the words she was waiting to hear.

"You're right, Millie! You're absolutely right." And reaching across the table I gave her hand a thankful squeeze, at the same time nodding my head in recognition and understanding. There was no point dwelling on and worrying about all the terrible things that could happen. What good did worrying do anyway? It was not going to help me and it was certainly not going to help Ky either.

Right there, right then, I knew what I needed to do and that was to focus on his recovery. That was what mattered most and it was up to me to help make it happen.

But although you can write the story in your head, life sometimes chooses its own path and its own outcomes. And those are not necessarily the ones that you, yourself had planned.

One thing is certain though, not in a million years did I anticipate what lay ahead.

A small miracle...

When I entered the school grounds the next morning, I attempted to push aside the feelings of guilt at the thought of continuing on with my daily existence. I'd made a promise to myself that I would maintain positive thoughts only but it was so much harder than I remembered. And taking a few deep breaths to quieten the anxiety that threatened just below the surface, I looked around for Millie.

The hallway was buzzing with students, deep in conversation over their weekend and the latest gossip. Glancing around at the many familiar faces, I felt as though I were in a bubble of sorts, in a world within a world. Unfortunately my world right then, felt isolated and alone. I looked out from the invisible screen surrounding me and all I could see were happy, smiling, contented faces. I could hear the loud voices filled with laughter and amusement. But my world was empty of all that. It was as though I'd just landed there from another place and another time.

It felt uncomfortable and surreal and I searched frantically for Millie. She was my support person, the one who would help me survive the reality I found myself in right then; one that was so vastly different from what I'd been consumed by at the hospital, just the day before. And after all, Millie was the one who had convinced me to go to school. If it hadn't been for her encouragement, I'd be back at the hospital sitting alongside Ky.

But where was she? We'd arranged to meet at the entrance to the school grounds, and so far she was nowhere to be seen.

Tired of standing and waiting alone, I headed inside the building to search for my other friends. I'd had phone calls the evening before, from Becky, Lisa and Jess as well as a couple of others who had obviously seen the evening news broadcast. But I felt so drained and exhausted that I just didn't have the strength or the energy to talk, and had given them a few details but that was all. Although very grateful for their support, the calls of sympathy were something I struggled to deal with right then, especially when I was trying my hardest to stay positive.

Then, out of the blue, I spotted Millie. From where I was standing, I could only see a glimpse. But it was the flick of her shining long dark hair that I recognized, before she disappeared from view once again.

Surrounded by a group of people in our grade, she appeared to be the center of attention, with girls and guys alike competing for a chance to talk to her. Taking in the scene in front of me, I realized immediately that I should have expected that very scenario. Millie had been away for a long time and naturally her friends would be excited to have her back. I also had to remind myself that after I'd moved to the country with my family, she had obviously continued on with her life. And in that time, it was clear that she'd become very popular.

What right did I have to expect things to go back to the way they once were? Back then, it had pretty much been Millie and I. Of course we'd had other friends, quite a big group actually, and that had included Blake and a few other girls and boys who we used to regularly hang out with. But essentially, it was just me and Millie, and in those days, we'd been inseparable.

Masking my disappointment, I headed for my own locker. It stood further down the hallway and I took a quick glance towards her as I passed by. Assuming she hadn't noticed me, I kept on walking, the leaden sensation in my stomach feeling heavier with every step.

And then I heard her voice.

"Julia!" she called loudly.

I could hear it distinctly above the din of loud chattering and laughter that surrounded her.

Looking back, I paused to flash a friendly smile and wave in recognition. But almost immediately, her attention was drawn once more to her friends who were clearly keen to continue their conversation.

Pulling my locker door open, I reached inside for the books I would need that morning. Glad to have something to occupy myself, I focused my attention on the inside of my locker. And then the bell rang. The loud clang vibrating throughout the building as the throng of noisy bustling students instantly began moving towards their classrooms; their chatter and cheery laughter not skipping a beat as they all made their way in unison to the classes that awaited them.

Heading to my own first class of the day, Science with Mr. Blandford, I passed Becky and Lisa who gave me a quick hug before promising to meet up during morning break at our usual lunchtime spot. Entering the classroom alone, I searched for a seat at the back of the room. And in the hope that by some stroke of luck, Millie might happen to appear at the doorway, I saved a seat next to mine just in case.

When everyone had filed in and taken their places, the hum of conversation was soon silenced when our teacher began to speak. With the time ticking on however, it was clear that Millie would not be arriving.

Just the day before we'd discussed the possibility of sharing classes. The timetable had changed somewhat in recent months due to an influx of new students, and there had been a shuffling of classes and teachers. So Millie was unsure as to how the changes affected her until she visited the office to finalize her new schedule.

Tuning out from Mr. Blandford's boring monologue, I scanned the classroom thoughtfully, images of Ky's smiling face and memories of the first time he'd sat alongside me in that very room, coming vividly to mind. Even though that had occurred so long ago, I could clearly remember the tingle of excitement I'd felt at the light touch of his fingers on mine when he had brushed against me. At the time I'd thought it accidental that he had reached for his pen and touched my hand instead. He later confided however, that it had been no accident at all.

Smiling at the memory, I felt my pulse quicken in response. The mere sight of him always caused my heart to race, let alone the feel of his skin on mine. His touch alone sent me into a frenzy I found difficult to control. Picturing in my mind a repetition of that scene, where we sat alongside one another, I felt the spark continuing to thrive. It was no wonder I was unable to concentrate on anything but him and wondered vaguely what sort of marks I'd end up with at the end of the semester.

But exams, assessments and grades were the least of my concerns right then as a vision of Ky laying alone in a hospital bed came flooding back. I just hoped that his grandmother would soon make her way there because I hated to think of him on his own.

In an attempt to jot down the notes Mr. Blandford had written on the board, I put my head down and tried to focus, but it was a task that I struggled to complete. Pen in hand, I scribbled on the page in front of me. However, rather than the words on the board, it was Ky's name that I scrawled over and over again inside my Science book.

Ky and Julia

Julia and Ky

So engrossed in the task, it was with a start that I noticed someone had abruptly sat down on the stool beside me. And looking up in stunned disbelief, I realized the scenario I'd hoped for had actually eventuated.

"Millie!" I exclaimed, the surprise evident in my voice. "Are you in this class?"

"Yes," she beamed delightedly. "They had me listed for Miss Foster's class but I asked if I could swap to this one!"

The simple realization that this had occurred flooded me with relief so immense, I was forced to blink away the tears. Even though we'd hoped for it to be the case, the chance that Millie might end up in my class was pretty slim especially as I knew that it was already full. But apparently, the parents of a girl who'd been away for ages had only just that morning, confirmed their daughter was now attending a private school in the district. So this created a space for Millie.

Although really only a minor incident, to me it seemed that a miracle had taken place and I was instantly flooded with reassurance that other miracles were also on the way. It was simply the best news and I shook my head in amazement.

After exchanging an excited hug, I attempted to focus on the lesson but I felt so happy at the turn of events, I barely comprehended a word Mr. Blandford said. Things were all going to work out, I was sure of it. And I was also sure that Millie's positive influence had something to do with that. It just seemed crazy that between the two of us, she seemed to be the positive one, whereas in the past, it had always been me. How things could change so dramatically was beyond me.

What mattered most right then though was the fact that Millie was there, and while we didn't get a chance to chat properly until the lesson ended, I was so happy to have her alongside me.

When the bell finally signaled the end of the lesson and we made our way to the classroom door, she turned towards me with an unexpected apology. "Sorry, I didn't get a chance to talk to you this morning, Julia. I haven't seen everyone for so long and they all wanted to catch up!"

"That's okay," I replied, with a smile. "I knew your friends would be keen to see you."

"You should come and sit with us during morning break," she continued. "They're all so nice, I know you'll love them."

I'd already mentioned the day before that I had become close friends with Becky, Lisa, Beth and Jess, and I was aware that it was going to be tricky as Millie hung out with a completely different group.

When I explained however, that I'd promised to meet up with the girls and tell them the full details of Ky's accident, she completely understood. I realized that it would also give her a chance to catch up properly with her own friends, so we agreed to see each other briefly after school before I headed to the hospital.

Then, when Millie later offered to come along while I visited Ky, once again I felt extremely grateful for her support.

And I soon discovered that without Millie, there was no way

I could have coped.

A turn of events...

It was just after the final bell of the day, that I received a text from Ky's grandmother, and I was sure that miracles were definitely taking place...

Julia, come as soon as you can. Ky is out of his coma!

Overwhelmed with excitement I could barely wait to reach the hospital, and as I ran with Millie to catch the early bus, I was reminded of days gone by, the image of the two of us clear in my head. On many occasions, we had raced frantically alongside one another, often late for a bus or an event but always in fits of laughter over a joke or something funny that one of us had shared. Back then, we'd experienced so many exciting and happy moments together, but it was quite clear there had never been one as important or as special as that very afternoon.

Ky was out of his coma. The news was so overpowering, so incredible and for me, the anticipation of seeing him almost too much to cope with!

When we arrived at the hospital, it was with a flurry of nerves that I led Millie towards the elevator that would take us to the wing where he was situated. My intention was to sneak Millie past the nurses' station in order for her to accompany me to his room. They were pretty strict on visitors and although visiting hours had officially commenced, they were still enforcing the family visitors' only rule for Ky. I was not actually a family member myself...it was only because of his grandmother's insistence that I was included on that small list.

As luck would have it though, we were able to make our way to his room without being noticed and I gently pushed his door open and peeked inside, expecting to see Mrs. Robertson sitting there, ready to welcome me.

Instead however, except for Ky himself, the room was deserted, and I felt an instantaneous joy at being given the chance to reunite with him without his grandmother looking on.

Millie had already suggested that she should wait outside, to give me some time alone with him before being introduced. And taking her up on the offer of privacy, I entered quietly in the hope of tip-toeing towards the bed and surprising him.

He was sitting up, looking out the nearby window and appeared to be totally engrossed in the view of the street beyond. As I made my way silently to his bedside, I could feel the smile stretch widely across my face, the excitement inside me almost bubbling over.

Noticing the movement in the room, he turned in my direction and stared, but before he could react further, I was already by his side with my arms wrapped gently around him.

"Ky!" I squealed, unable to contain the excitement I was feeling. "Ky, you're awake!!"

Taking a step back, I stroked his hair as I sat gently down on the bed beside him. I had to touch him, to feel the life within him and ensure that the vision in front of me was real.

It was a miracle, and this time, a major one. The only signs of injury appeared to be the obvious scrapes and bruises along with a broken arm which was secured by a hard plaster cast. And although he was attached to the one remaining machine that still stood at the side of his bed, I could see that my prayers had definitely been answered. Overcome with gratitude and thanks, I hugged him gently once more.

"Oh my gosh, Ky," the words tumbled from my lips. Delirious with happiness and relief, I could not contain the joy inside me. "We've been so worried about you. But I knew you'd wake up. I knew you would!"

With the realization that I was overwhelming him, I took a step back, pausing for a moment to take in the confused expression on his face. His brow was creased in a slight frown and the small smile at the corner of his mouth was certainly not the reaction I was expecting to see.

"Ky?" I stammered. "Ky, are you okay?"

It was then that I heard the door creak slowly open behind me and I turned to see his grandmother standing there, the smile wide on her face.

"Julia! It's so good you're here! Ky's come back to us, Julia. He's come back!"

Grinning in acknowledgement, I looked at her and then towards Millie who had entered the room behind her, the look of delight obvious on her face as well.

But when I turned back to Ky, it was the questioning stare that he was directing towards his grandmother that created an instant anxiety in the pit of my stomach. It seemed clear to me right then that something was definitely wrong.

"Ky," Mrs. Roberson asked, the concern in her voice indicating that she too, could see there was a problem. "Are you okay?"

Very gently, I reached for his hand. But instantly, he pulled away, clearly uncomfortable with the gesture. Fear took its place inside me. I looked into his eyes, those beautiful gray-blue eyes that I loved and adored, and the guarded stare that peered cautiously back, filled me with dread.

"Ky," I prodded gently, "It's me, Julia. And this is my friend, Millie. The one who has just returned from overseas. You remember me talking about her, don't you?"

But the confusion was clear on his face, and he shook his head slightly, his brow creasing into a deep frown.

It was then that he opened his mouth to speak. "Ah, sorry, do I know you?"

Struggling to breathe, I felt the knot in my stomach take a firm hold, the tension tightening as the seconds ticked by.

"Ky, it's me, Julia. Of course you know me!"

I uttered the words forcefully. This had to be a joke of some sort. But why he would choose this moment was something I could not understand. It was not funny at all. In fact it was cruel and I didn't like it one little bit.

Glancing quickly at his grandmother did nothing to ease the anxious beat of my pounding heart. It throbbed wildly in my chest as I stared white-faced at him once more.

He was staring back at me. The blank look of unfamiliarity towards the identity of the girl in front of him blatantly clear.

Alarm bells rang in my mind and the sound began to work its way through my veins, desperate to escape and be heard. My hand moved in an automatic response towards my mouth. It seemed a helpless attempt to block the noise that threatened to explode into the room.

Once more the grip of doom, had taken over.

And I was powerless to prevent it.

Confusion...

Staring at Millie, aghast, I was lost for words. How could he not know me? How could that be possible, when only a few days before, he'd told me how special I was?

"You're amazing, Julia."

They had been his exact words as we'd sat by side after school one afternoon, his hand on mine and the butterflies turning crazy cartwheels inside me.

But that vivid memory was quickly washed away when I recalled his grandmother's voice, the growing concern obvious on her face.

"Ky, this is Julia. You remember Julia, don't you?"

His smile broadened then, and I felt the tension in my body relax ever so slightly. Surely, it was just a minor memory lapse. Of course he knew me. I'm the girl he loves, aren't I? How on earth could he forget me?

And then, with a shake of his head, he opened his mouth to speak once more.

"I'm sorry but I don't think I've ever met you before."

Pacing the floor of the doctor's office a little while later, my head spun. It was simply too much to comprehend.

"Amnesia can sometimes occur after a head injury," the doctor tried to explain. "Hopefully his memory will gradually return, but it could take some time. All we can do is wait and see."

The hysteria had risen in my voice and I struggled to remain calm. I was on the verge of losing all control and had to force myself to pause in order to take a deep breath before speaking again.

"But he seems perfectly fine except for the fact that he thinks I'm a stranger! He knows his grandmother and his brother. He knows who he is, where he lives and where he goes to school. If he knows all of that, why doesn't he know me?"

"Head injuries can cause different types of amnesia," the doctor continued, his quiet, matter of fact tone causing my frustration to reach boiling point.

"It appears that he has no recollection of the accident whatsoever. When I asked him what he last remembers, he said it was his brother's birthday. He recalls the day vividly as though it were yesterday. The problem is, that day occurred nearly 10 months ago but Ky thinks it has only just happened."

"I don't understand," I stammered, with a confused shake of my head. "What are you saying?"

With a sigh, the doctor continued. "Usually this sort of thing is temporary. We just need to be patient and hopefully his full memory will return. But at this point in time, it appears that Ky has lost all memory of the past 10 months of his life."

Focus...

As I paced the floor of my bedroom, I felt sick beyond measure. Ky didn't know me. He had no idea who I was. Apart from that, everything else about him seemed absolutely fine. The doctor said they'd have to do more tests and in the meantime, all they could do was continue to monitor his progress.

I left him there, in the hospital room along with his grandmother. It would be several days before he'd be allowed to go home and the doctor suggested that I return the next afternoon, in the hope that my appearance would spark a memory so that it would all come flowing back.

That was the way it usually worked, he told me. Apparently, it might just take one person, or a photo or the mention of an event, and the memories would begin to return.

Millie had done her best to comfort me and if she hadn't been there I would not have managed. Thankfully Matt came to pick us up as soon as I texted him. But the minute I saw him hop out of his car, I became a sobbing mess. He looked helplessly towards me and then at Millie, the fear evident in his eyes. Obviously he was thinking the worst.

I had left the explanation to Millie. I didn't want to talk about it at all. Instead I just hugged him tightly, the whole time wishing desperately that it was simply a bad dream that I'd soon awake from. Surely that had to be the case.

But later on in the privacy of my bedroom, the question repeated itself over and over again. Why? Why did this have to happen? My mind raced with recent images of the two of us together and I pictured his beautiful, wonderful, mesmerizing smile; the one he'd flashed the moment he spotted me calling from the side of the road behind him. It had only lasted a second. Then the car had hit him and his precious smile was gone.

Recalling that scene made me want to vomit. I'd been keeping it in the recesses of my mind, unwilling to witness it all over again. It was simply too horrific, the graphic details too upsetting to think about. But right then, I could not let it go. It remained there in full view and on constant replay, flashing vividly in my thoughts over and over and over.

Then, almost as if she knew I needed her, my phone rang. The shrill sound instantly bringing me back and causing the disturbing scene in my mind to disappear.

Reaching for the phone with one hand, I wiped the sweat from my brow with the other and moved towards the window. Taking a gulp of fresh air, I felt the nausea subside somewhat, along with my whirlwind of wild thoughts.

"Julia, are you okay?"

Just the sound of Millie's voice was enough to calm me, the reassurance I desperately needed right then coming from the other end of the phone line, as it stretched in an invisible thread and connected me to her.

"Millie," I responded, and thankful tears sprang instantly to the corners of my eyes.

Blinking them away, I sat down on the bed and took in her words. "He'll be fine, Julia. You heard the doctor. It's just going to be temporary. Stay positive and focus on what you want to happen."

Nodding my head with acceptance, I stared at myself in the

mirror. Then taking a deep breath, I replied. "Yes, Millie. He will be fine. His memory will come back. Everything will be okay."

And once more, I pictured the two of us together…his hand in mine and his warm smile.

That was the outcome I needed to focus on.

Surely that was what lay ahead.

And it was up to me to make it happen.

Prayers...

The next day at school seemed endless. I stared at the clock on the wall of each class countless times during every lesson, willing the hands to move more quickly. I was desperate to get to the hospital, desperate to find out if Ky's memory had returned or even parts of it, with flashes of our time together coming back to him.

I created a vision in my mind and it was of the familiar beautiful smile appearing on his face the moment he saw me, along with the words, "Julia, it's so good to see you! Where have you been?"

If I'd had my way, I would have returned to see him first thing in the morning, but his grandmother had insisted that I go to school.

"The doctors will be doing tests throughout most of the day, Julia. And I think he needs some recovery time alone. It would be best if you arrive later in the afternoon. Hopefully by then we will see some progress."

I accepted her decision, knowing full well that she was right. And I also knew that school would be the distraction I needed. It was soon apparent as well, that I had the support I wanted and hoped for from my friends, all of whom listened intently to the latest developments.

Their initial reaction had been one of astonishment as they tried to come to terms with the situation I'd been confronted with at the hospital the day before.

"OMG! That is awful!! You poor thing, Julia!" Becky's look was of genuine sympathy as she shook her head in acknowledgement of what I was going through. "It must've been such a shock when you realized he didn't even know who you were!"

"The whole thing is crazy!" Beth commented dramatically. "How can someone wake up one day with the past 10 months of their life completely erased from their memory banks? I just don't get it!"

"Surely though, it will all come back. I mean the guy is in love with you," Lisa's persuasive tone showed the conviction she felt. "We've all seen the way he looks at you. He adores you, Julia. It's obvious! And there's no way that he could forget you. This will only be temporary, I'm sure of it!"

Grateful for their encouragement, I took in every word, each positive comment helping to build my own self-belief.

But it was with anxiety and unease that I entered the foyer of the hospital later that afternoon and made my way through the building towards his room. When I gently opened his door however, and peeked tentatively inside, I was quite surprised to find it empty. His unmade bed and belongings still cluttered the small space but he and his grandmother were nowhere to be seen.

After taking a glance in each direction of the hallway only to find the area deserted, apart from a visitor making her way towards the exit located at the end of the corridor, I decided to just go into the room and wait.

As I stepped inside and looked around, the lone arm chair still sitting idly in the corner opposite, beckoned me. Heading towards it, I took comfort in its familiarity, the many hours I'd already spent cocooned within its arms, creating a mild sense of security.

The time spent in that very spot just staring at the unresponsive boy laying comatose in the nearby bed had made me accustomed to waiting. But after about 30 minutes had ticked by and still there was no sign of Ky, or anyone else for that matter, I began to fidget with uncomfortable impatience.

Leaning back on the headrest behind me, I closed my eyes for a moment, only to quickly open them again as a sudden thought jolted me upright. I'd promised Ky's friends at school that I would pass on their messages of support, which of course I would do. What I neglected to tell them though was that Ky didn't know who I was. Although I'd told my close friends, it wasn't something that I really wanted anyone else to know. Not yet anyway. And besides that, I'd been focusing on the idea of his memory returning.

His group of friends had been keen to make a visit to the hospital until I mentioned that for the time being, only 'family' were allowed. My concern however, was based around how much he would remember about his life at Carindale High School. And what his response would be when he saw his friends. Would he remember that particular group or not? He'd been a student there for quite some time and it had occurred to me in an abrupt flash, that I may be the only one from school who he didn't recognize.

Deep in thought, I turned to look out the window, where the curtains had been drawn to allow a full view of the street outside. Doing my best to push aside all negativity, I focused on the park across the road where a variety of people were enjoying the last of the warm sunshine that the afternoon had unexpectedly provided. There had been a huge downpour of rain earlier that morning but the welcome change in the weather had obviously encouraged everyone to be outdoors.

Children ran through the playground while parents sat by and watched. At the same time, passers-by continued on their way, that particular park was obviously a popular place for an afternoon stroll or bike ride. And I focused my attention on the scene, unnoticed from my perch above as the myriad of people proceeded with their daily existence, blissfully unaware of the turmoil that was attempting to envelope the room where I sat.

Sighing deeply, I turned my gaze back towards my surroundings and the unmade bed in front of me; to the place where Ky had spent so much time, unconscious and completely unaware of what had occurred only hours earlier.

Then, as images of his recovery came to mind, I forced myself to consider a different outlook entirely. I needed to be thankful, I realized abruptly. Grateful for the miracle that he had actually survived…that was what I had prayed for and it had happened. He was walking and talking and apart from a memory lapse, he seemed barely unaffected by the turn of events. For that I knew I should be very thankful.

As Millie and the other girls had already tried to convince me, his memory would return. It had to. The concept was just too bizarre for any other outcome to even become a possibility.

Miracles were created every day. I knew it.

And I prayed for one to occur right there, in that very room, the minute he walked in.

If he smiles, it will be a sign; a sign that his memory is coming back. The thought raced around in my head and I played the scene over and over. The vision was clear, as I sat waiting, all the while willing his smiling face to appear.

Then, just as I made a move to stand and go in search of the boy I loved, my impatience too great to wait any longer, I saw the door knob turn. And frozen with hope, I looked on, breathless and anxious, as the door began to slowly swing open in a wide arc towards me.

Patience…

I stared out the car window to the street beyond. The houses flashed by in a blur as the radio blasted one of the latest hit songs. It was a particular favorite and normally, I would sing along, the lyrics etched so firmly in my memory that I was able to remember every word.

But although I didn't feel like singing right then, I was grateful for the distraction. So much so, that I'd reached over to turn up the volume. Anything to avoid having to make conversation right then. I was sure that Matt was grateful also; the silence between us as he drove towards our house had become more and more awkward, so the loud music was a good excuse not to talk.

Straight away he had known. The moment he'd arrived to pick me up from the hospital, he was aware of what had happened. It was written all over my face and he didn't even have to ask.

Just like the pages of a book, my expression had told the story. But just in case he'd misread the meaning, I told him anyway.

"No, he doesn't remember me. And the doctors have no idea when his memory will come back. They said we just have to wait and see."

Without saying a word in reply, he had reached towards me and I could feel the warmth of his strong muscular arms as he wrapped them firmly around my shoulders. It was one of those special brother-sister moments that don't happen very often. Neither of us needed to speak. There was nothing to say. The strength and comfort in his hug said so much more than words ever could. And right then, I think I felt closer to him than ever before.

Feeling the tears begin to fall, I brushed them quickly away and turned towards the car. Without even reaching for the handle, the door opened, almost magically. And then I realized that Matt had opened it for me. Such a small gesture, but one that I'd never seen from my brother before, not for me anyway. That movement in itself spoke volumes.

When I made my way into the house, it was as though a kind of numbness had taken hold and all I wanted was to be alone.

Walking into the kitchen, I was hit with the aroma of his favorite meal, spaghetti and meat sauce, which he'd told me he had already prepared for dinner. It was actually one of the few meals that he knew how to cook and his version was one that I particularly enjoyed. But not that night. That night I had no appetite whatsoever.

Turning to him gratefully, I thanked him for the ride home and for cooking dinner and for just being there.

"That's okay," he said quietly, the concern clear on his face.

And then, in an effort to reassure me once more, he continued, "Don't worry, Julia. His memory will come back. It has to."

With a weak smile in response, I trudged up the stairs to my room and closed the door quietly behind me. Without bothering to reply to the many texts that had appeared on my phone, I switched it off and laid down on my bed. I wasn't at all sleepy, I just wanted to be alone with my thoughts; the vision of Ky when he had appeared in his hospital room firmly embedded in my head.

Immediately, I'd realized. The very moment I saw him, I was aware that nothing had changed. And his hesitant expression at the sight of me sitting there waiting, hurt more than anything.

In place of the warm and welcoming smile that I'd so desperately hoped for was the familiar frown that told me everything I needed to know.

Even though his grandmother had tried to gently prod him in an attempt to bring some memories back, he had shaken his head in dismay.

And not wanting to upset him further, I had left the room. He was clearly uncomfortable with me being there and I could see that my own visibly distraught reaction was only making things worse.

His doctor told me that it was essential to take things slowly. One day at a time he said.

"Apart from his broken arm and the memory loss, he seems to be recovering very well. So I see no reason why he can't return to school next week. Perhaps that will also help to stimulate his memories. That could be just the trigger he needs."

And so I had to cling to the hope that on his return to school, everything would go back to normal. His face would light up every time he saw me and rather than the stare of a stranger, he would move quickly towards me with that beautiful smile that I loved so much.

That was what I had to focus on. And fighting away the concern that I'd be one of the few people at school who he did not remember, I concentrated on Millie's words, repeating them once more in my head, "You get what you focus on!"

And so, I spent the hours that followed, attempting to visualize in my mind, the image I wanted to see in real life.

This was constantly interrupted however, by the persistent sound of the downstairs phone which continued to ring. To begin with, Matt had climbed the stairs to my door, quietly opening it to see if I was awake and able to take the call, which was obviously from someone ringing for an update. But I pretended to be asleep and waited impatiently for him to close the door again. Although grateful that so many people cared, I was in no mood to talk and decided to let Matt tell them the details. After all, there wasn't too much to report, was there?

Ky didn't remember me. It was as simple as that.

From my bedroom, I could hear Matt's muffled voice on the phone downstairs and was able to make out the identity of each caller and the basics of his conversation. Each time the dialogue was pretty much the same. Except for when Dad rang. That phone call was much longer than the rest and I could hear Matt's convincing tone, reassuring Dad that he'd keep an eye on me.

"I'll be okay," I thought to myself. "I just need to be patient."

That was what the doctor had said before I left the hospital, his voice gentle but firm as he patted me sympathetically on the shoulder.

And then I'd made my way via the long corridors of the hospital and down the stairs to wait for Matt to arrive, all the while, desperately trying to fend off the fear that clung tightly to the pit of my stomach. I could still feel it there, several hours later, as I tossed and turned in my bed. That nauseating sick feeling of dread.

Yes, his memory may come back. And yes, that was what I

needed to focus on.

But what if it never returned? What if he was never able to recall our time together?

What would happen then?

Unwelcome news…

When Ky returned to school the following week, I watched from afar, too nervous and anxious to approach him. I hadn't been back to the hospital at all since my previous visit. After all, what was the point? My presence only seemed to agitate him, and the whole scenario was just too upsetting for me to even contemplate. So I took his grandmother's advice and decided to give him some space; hoping of course that he might call or text me. But that never happened. I didn't hear a word.

During that time though, I did some research. Lots of it. And instead of studying for my upcoming exams, I spent hours searching the Internet for some insight into Ky's condition.

Initially, I'd begun to feel slightly more at ease. The more I searched, the more I felt convinced that his memory loss would only be temporary. Apparently amnesia was very common for people with head injuries and while some forgot only a few minutes of their experiences prior to an accident, others lost a much bigger chunk. However, as each person's recovery took place, the memories tended to return.

I tried to convince myself that this would be the case with Ky. But when the days passed by and there was still no word of any progress, I began to feel doubtful.

This feeling was worsened when his grandmother called to give me an update; one that did nothing to improve my outlook. Unfortunately the news was not good as there had been no improvement whatsoever. And that was when I really started to worry.

"I've mentioned your name a few times, Julia and talked about some of the things that you've done together. But Ky has no recollection at all."

I stood listening to her gentle voice on the other end of the phone, but all I could do was utter a deep sigh, the disappointment in my voice was raw.

"Don't worry, darling," she continued. "I'm sure that once he's back at school, all the pieces of the puzzle will begin to fit together."

It was after that phone call that I decided to do another internet search, desperate to look for something I could do to help. It was time to become proactive. Surely there was something that could be done to help bring the memories back. But rather than finding a cure, I managed to locate an article that described something else entirely and it was information that I wished I hadn't found at all.

The article was a doctor's account of various patients he had treated, each of whom had suffered from a condition known as retrograde amnesia, which is the official term for Ky's type of memory loss. The article had gone on to explain that the less severe a head injury was, the better the chance of a full recovery.

However, in one particular incident where a man was hit by a speeding car and suffered a very traumatic blow to the head, an accident that sounded very similar to Ky's, the man lost all memory of the previous 12 months of his life. Several years later, it still hadn't returned.

That was when I began to feel ill. 12 months! A full 12 months of memories that had been wiped, never to be remembered again.

The hands of fear clutched tightly at my stomach once more. And it was with dread that I made my way to school the following day, where as soon as I hopped off the bus, I spotted Ky's blue car parked adjacent to the bus stop, in its usual place in the school carpark.

The scene felt surreal; it was as though nothing out of the ordinary had occurred and that everything would go on as before.

But that was a pipe dream.

Because something very extraordinary had happened and how on earth could everything go on as it once had?

The worst part was though, I had absolutely no idea of what I could do to fix it.

The way we were…

Science class. My first lesson of the day and the one class that Ky and I shared.

Anxiously, I made my way through the open doorway and searched for a seat at the back of the room, half hoping that he wouldn't notice me when he walked in but also hoping on the other hand, that he would.

Unfortunately though, Millie hadn't arrived at school yet. She had texted me earlier to say that she was going to be late and probably wouldn't arrive until morning break. I couldn't believe my luck! If ever I needed her beside me, it was definitely right then.

Placing my backpack on the seat beside me, to prevent anyone from trying to claim it, I pretended to be looking inside it for something I'd misplaced. Although it was quite clear that my books and pens were all sitting on the bench top in front of me, I needed an excuse to occupy the chair so that it was available for Ky, just in case he chose to sit there. As anxious as I was, that was what I was really hoping for.

The lesson that day included a variety of experiments that we had to do in groups and Mr. Blandford already had the necessary equipment set up in preparation for us to use. Several kids had arranged themselves in readiness while others were still trying to get organized. In an attempt to avoid eye contact with anyone, I continued to focus on the contents of my bag when unexpectedly, I heard a male voice calling my name.

Looking towards the sound that had come from the front of

the room, my heart momentarily skipped a beat. That was until I realized it wasn't Ky who was calling out to me at all, but a boy named Jasper who was beckoning me to join him and the others at his table. It appeared that they were one person short and it was either me who they could ask or a very unpopular boy called Oliver.

Realizing that I had no other choice but to join them, I made my way towards the front and pulled up a stool alongside Jasper. Then, just as Mr. Blandford began to explain the procedure we were to follow, Ky walked into the room.

With my heart pounding wildly I glanced away, too nervous and embarrassed to even look at him. It seemed to be the most awkward moment of my life and I could not believe that it was happening. My so-called "boyfriend" had entered the class and I completely avoided making any sort of eye contact whatsoever.

What was wrong with me? Was that how I was going to handle the whole situation, by looking away every time he happened to be nearby? They were the thoughts racing through my head as I tried to focus on what the teacher was saying, but I found it impossible to concentrate.

Meanwhile, Ky had been directed by Mr. Blandford to take a seat at the table near ours so he could join Oliver and a couple of others who had also just arrived. Without trying to be obvious, I took a quick glance in his direction but he seemed focused on the teacher and what he was saying. It appeared quite clear that he hadn't even noticed me.

From where I was seated though, I was able to keep an eye on him while pretending to listen to Mr. Blandford as he explained the instructions. That was, until I saw everyone in my group leave their seats in order to gather around the equipment that had been placed at the opposite end of our table.

Apparently, we'd just been given permission to begin the experiment which involved testing the chemical reaction of various liquids when combined together. We also needed to heat some of the mixtures using a Bunsen burner and take note of the results. The issue for me however, was that I had no idea of the procedure as I had not listened to a word Mr. Blandford had just said.

Then, to make matters worse, the others in my group decided to assign me as the note taker which I found frustrating because that job required concentration, something I was really struggling with right then. Instead, all I wanted to do was focus on Ky.

Soon realizing that this was just not going to work, I picked up my notebook in defeat and moved myself to a position where I could easily view what the others were doing. Then, taking notes as requested, I gradually became more involved in the activity and apart from the odd glance in Ky's direction, was able to do a reasonable job. At least I hoped so, as everyone was relying on the fact that I'd jotted down the findings accurately. Without accurate notes, it would be very difficult to complete the follow-up report due later in the week.

When finally the lesson ended and I was able to make my way out the classroom door and into the corridor, I glanced quickly around in the hope that Ky might still be nearby. However, everyone seemed to be taking the opportunity for a quick chat in the hallway before our next class, and the area had become quite crowded. Just as I was about to move away, I heard his distinctive voice amidst the loud chatter. But when I followed the sound that I'd recognized so easily, much to my surprise, I found him deep in conversation with Jackie Armstrong.

The reason I found this unusual was that prior to his accident, Ky would often roll his eyes at Jackie and her group of friends, clearly not impressed by their attention seeking behavior. Jackie in particular was renowned for being a serious flirt and had a reputation for chasing and then dumping every good looking guy she came across. Apparently, Ky had been on her target list at one stage but back then, he had not been in the least bit interested.

From what I could see though, this was not the case anymore as he seemed completely taken in by the coy expression that was glued to her face while she laughed and fussed over whatever he was saying. Perhaps it was my imagination running wild and I'd misread the situation, but I was not at all comfortable with watching the two of them together.

With pangs of jealousy clawing relentlessly inside me, I turned abruptly in the opposite direction and headed towards my next class, the sick feeling in my stomach becoming worse with every step.

Later that morning, when the bell finally rang for morning recess, I headed outside to my usual lunch spot where I had arranged to meet Millie. Over the past week, she had been choosing to spend at least one break with my group of friends each day. This way she was able to hang out with me as well as her own friends, which seemed to suit everyone. And for this I was very grateful.

That morning however, I still hadn't had a chance to talk to Ky. But the moment I sat down in the lunch area alongside Millie, everything suddenly changed.

"OMG!" she whispered frantically. "Look who's heading this way."

The second I followed her gaze and realized that Ky was walking towards us, I could feel my stomach drop. It seemed that for me, an anxiety attack had become the usual scenario whenever I saw him, or whenever his name was mentioned. And that particular instance was no exception.

Quickly averting my eyes, I forced myself to focus on the sandwich in my lap; the thought of him in my sights causing my head to spin and a flood of sweat to break out on my hands and forehead.

"OMG! OMG! OMG!" I muttered the words quietly under my breath, all the while keeping my eyes downcast as I listened to his approaching footsteps crunching noisily on the gravel path and getting louder with every step. Then just as I thought he was going to walk straight past, I heard Millie speak.

"Hi Ky. How are you?"

Her voice was loud and clear and there was no way for him to walk by without acknowledging us. I wasn't sure exactly what he had intended, but he had no choice except to stop and talk.

Looking up, I could feel the flush of red on my face which I was sure deepened into an even brighter shade when Millie suggested that he sit down and join us. Shuffling along slightly to make room, she patted the seat next to her, indicating that he should sit there. It was the only vacant spot and I watched in disbelief as she babbled on. Obviously it was an attempt to ease the awkwardness of the moment, but I was in awe of the way she was able to chatter on as if absolutely nothing was wrong and everything was as it should be.

I couldn't help but notice Ky's look of discomfort, probably due to the fact that I was there. But with Millie's incessant chatter, he appeared to relax somewhat. Her outgoing and friendly nature soon had him joining in the conversation and the tension in his face appeared to gradually melt away.

All the while, however, I sat listening in but saying very little. And Ky pretty much avoided all eye contact with me. The whole time, he just focused on Millie's conversation and although she tried to include me, I'd become shy and introverted, unable to find the words I needed or wanted to say.

His memory loss was not mentioned. Millie avoided the topic and so did he. It seemed to be an unspoken taboo and although I was desperate to at least refer to it, the words remained unspoken. Deep down though, I already knew the answer. And while I did not want to admit it, beyond all doubt, I knew.

When I looked into his eyes, there was no sign of any connection between us. None whatsoever. And when the bell rang a short time later, he stood quickly, taking the opportunity to excuse himself and head back to class.

Looking at Millie in despair, I tried desperately to prevent the tears from falling. If I started crying, I was sure I would not be able to stop.

Ky seemed fully recovered. Apart from his broken arm, everything else about him appeared to be completely normal. Everything that was, except his relationship with me.

Would his memory ever return? Would we ever go back to being the way we were such a short time ago? Would he ever again smile that wonderful smile while looking at me?

Too many questions.

Questions that I was petrified of learning the answers to.

Feelings…

As the days progressed, nothing seemed to change. I went to classes each day, hung out with Millie and the others during breaks, and watched Ky from a distance…always from a distance.

There were several times that we passed each other in the corridors, heading to and from classes, but the atmosphere between us was awkward. There were even a few occasions where I watched him purposely turn to talk to one of his friends in order to avoid me.

How could it be so hard to have a simple conversation? The whole situation was just too strange to even comprehend. One thing I did notice though was that he seemed to be getting a lot of attention from other girls. Whether that was always the case, I had no idea. Only having met him a few months earlier, I didn't know what went on beforehand as he had never really said very much about past girlfriends.

The attention from other girls was something I should not have been surprised about as he was so good looking. After all, his looks were what had attracted me in the first place. Those gorgeous features that lit up whenever he smiled were simply too special to ignore. It really was no wonder that so many girls were interested in him.

Funnily enough though, all this attention did not appear to faze him. And it certainly did not seem to be going to his head. Although he obviously took an interest in a few girls in particular, something that I was finding difficult to come to terms with, I could see that he was often unaware that so much female attention was being directed towards him. And that simple fact just made me love him even more.

Although he was clearly disinterested in my existence right then, I still had deep feelings for him. And all I could do was push through each day and live in hope that his memory would return. There was nothing I could do except hope and pray for things to go back to the way they once were.

And then one day, everything changed.

Unexpected encounter...

It was the week before the most exciting event of our school year, the Tenth Grade camp to Kappa Falls Outdoor Education Center. This was something that the entire grade had been looking forward to since the very beginning of junior high school. However, with everything going on recently, I'd hardly had a chance to give it much thought and I now desperately needed to get organized.

Thankfully, my friends had been planning for a while and I'd arranged to meet up with them during our lunch break so they could help me with all the last minute details. The best part was that Millie had decided to join our cabin group and for me, this was the coolest thing ever. I could hardly wait for the week to pass so that camp could begin. Obviously it was an awesome way for everyone to end the year but for me personally, it was exactly the distraction I needed.

Heading quickly along the corridor, I was keen to reach the lunch area where I knew the girls would be waiting. I strode purposefully along, deep in thought about the camp ahead when I was stopped by the sight of my Geography teacher, Mrs. Greene, struggling with a pile of boxes that she was carrying. Without thinking, I stopped to offer some assistance.

"Do you need some help, Mrs. Greene?"

The moment the words left my mouth, I regretted them.

"Yes please, Julia," she replied gratefully. "I really do need some help with these. They have to be taken to the main storage room on the other side of the campus and I was trying to avoid making two trips. I've asked the janitor several times to do it for me, but sometimes if you want a job done, you just have to do it yourself. If you wouldn't mind helping me that would be great!"

I knew for sure, that by the time I walked all the way over to that building and back, my lunch break would be over. As luck would have it, I'd already been held up by my English teacher who wanted to discuss the first draft of an essay that I'd handed in to be checked. While I was thankful for the feedback, I was conscious of the girls waiting for me and I had to mask my impatience while trying to pay attention to Miss Bromley's comments regarding my assignment.

As is often the case though, some plans are destined to go astray and I soon found out that I was in the midst of one of those days where every encounter seemed to be leading me in a different direction.

Realizing that I could hardly have walked past Mrs. Greene without offering to help, I begrudgingly accepted the fact that I was probably not going to be able to meet Millie and the others after all. So, with a discreet but frustrated sigh, I took hold of the uppermost boxes from the pile that she was carrying and headed down the walkway alongside her, all the while attempting to take part in her friendly conversation about the camp that I was still so unprepared for. Then, in mid-sentence, she was interrupted by the sound of her mobile phone.

Pulling it from her pocket, she stopped to answer the call while attempting to juggle the armful of boxes with her other hand. All the while, I stood impatiently by, waiting for her to finish speaking. However, when she ended the call, her expression had turned to one of obvious concern.

"I'm so sorry, Julia," she explained in a rush. "There's been some sort of emergency and I'm needed at the office. Do you think you could manage to take these on your own?"

Without waiting for an answer, she hurried on, "If you leave them tucked inside the building, just outside the storage room door that would be great. I'll head over there later to put them away."

It seemed then, that in the blink of an eye she had disappeared and I was left to deal with the boxes on my own.

"Don't worry about me," I muttered irritably under my breath. "I'll just carry them all for you! I don't care about missing my lunch break!"

Staring in frustration at the pile of boxes she had just dumped on the floor at my feet, I wondered how I was going to manage by myself.

"Typical!" Unable to control my annoyance, I spat the word loudly, not caring if anyone heard.

With a shake of my head and another frustrated sigh, I tried to comprehend how I'd managed to get myself into such a situation in the first place. Especially when all I wanted to do was meet Millie and the other girls for lunch!

All self-control deserting me completely, I kicked angrily at one of the boxes with the toe of my shoe. And then somehow resisted the temptation to kick it with full strength, just like a football towards a goal post, down the entire length of the hallway. If I damaged the box and the contents inside, that would just lead to more problems and I definitely didn't need that to happen.

In the hope of finding someone to help, I scanned the

hallway in each direction but there was no one in sight. Clearly, everyone was at lunch. So, with no other alternative, I crouched down in an attempt to gather all the boxes together so I could pick them up in one go. However, this proved to be useless as one box after another kept sliding off the top of the pile and onto the floor.

Becoming more and more frustrated by the second, I continued to stoop down in order to pick them up, only to find another box would fall off the top and join the others. Just when I was about to give it all up, in what seemed a bizarre twist of fate, I heard a voice call my name.

It was one of those moments that catches a person completely unaware. And later that evening when I had time to reflect on the chance meeting, I thought that maybe it was my reward for offering to help Mrs. Greene. And maybe, just maybe, it was a sign that my inner most prayers had been answered.

"You look like you need some help!"

I turned abruptly to the sound of the familiar voice and immediately my pulse began to quicken.

"I just passed Mrs. Greene," he continued in a friendly manner, "And she asked me to help you."

The sight of Ky heading in my direction was like a gift from the heavens. And in addition, the other miraculous occurrence was not so much the fact that he'd offered to help, but the manner in which he'd spoken to me. Those few words were probably the most that I'd heard from him since the accident, and by far the friendliest.

A small but nervous smile had formed on my face and I stood staring at him, not sure how to respond. Then, without another word, he reached towards me and took a pile of boxes out of my hands.

"I'd take more," he said, the grin on his own face widening, "But it's a bit hard with this cast on my arm. I can't wait to get it off!"

Forcing myself not to be awkward, which was something I'd become so good at whenever he was around, I smiled in return, a genuine smile of thanks. It was my chance to spend a few minutes with him, even though it only involved carrying boxes for the Geography teacher and I was determined not to spoil it.

Then, in a sudden rush of recognition, I stood motionless for a moment as I recalled abruptly that the two of us had been in that exact same situation on a previous occasion not so long ago.

"What's wrong?" he asked, curiously.

"Oh nothing, it's just that this reminds me of another time…." And then I stopped, faltering uncomfortably.

"Another time?" he questioned, his brow creasing into an inquisitive frown.

Then comprehension dawned. "Have we done this before?" he laughed, looking curiously at me.

With a deep breath, I nodded my head. I'd been unsure whether I should mention the day that the two of us had been asked to help a teacher out in much the same manner. That had been just after I'd first met Ky and now, quite coincidentally, the scenario had been repeated, so much so that it was almost an exact replica, with me feeling just as nervous the second time around.

But, determined not to ruin the opportunity to be with him, I searched for something to say, while at the same time he appeared to be doing exactly the same thing.

"Julia," he said abruptly, his tone becoming much more serious. "I'm sorry that I've been avoiding you."

Taken aback at the sound of his unexpected words, I felt my eyes being drawn to his, and instantly my heart melted. The beautiful pools of blue intensity that stared towards me in return, held me captive, and I was powerless to look away.

"That's okay." I murmured quietly, not sure how else to respond.

"No, it's not. I've been really rude to you." The abruptness of his reply caught me by surprise and I stood silently waiting for him to continue.

"Julia, I'm truly sorry! It's just that this whole thing has totally freaked me out. I've had no idea how to handle it."

He blurted the words quickly, the pain and frustration of the past few weeks showing clearly on his face. It was as though he had only just summed up the courage to confront the truth.

"I understand." Overwhelmed by a sudden burst of sympathy, my heart went out to him. "This must be so hard for you, Ky. I can only imagine what you're going through."

My voice shook with emotion as I spoke. It was as though I'd been struck a sudden blow. The clarity was instant, and finally, I understood the depth of the situation. Ever since the accident, I'd been filled with self-pity and misery so intense, that I had not even considered the overall impact on him. Completely self-absorbed, I had only thought of myself, so much so that I'd actually begun to resent him.

How could he not remember me?

Did I mean so little to him?

How could he go on with his life as if nothing had happened?

They were the thoughts that had continued to race around in my head, with little empathy at all for the pain and trauma that he was going through. But in that instant, I understood, and for the first time since the accident I felt the leaden sensation in the depths of my soul become a little lighter.

Then, as we made our way along the walkway that led to the rear of the school campus, we talked. And we continued to talk and then talked some more. We spoke about the events of that terrible day and then the aftermath when he'd woken from the coma, oblivious to who I was. He was open and honest and told me that apart from the driver of the car that had hit him, there was no one else to blame. It had been an accident and that was all.

He then told me about the counseling sessions which had become a regular part of his routine, in the hope that some of his memories may be triggered. The sessions were also designed to help him come to terms with the fact that for him, a huge chunk of his past had ceased to exist. It was just someone else's recount of a series of events that had he had no recollection of.

And when he asked about me and how I was feeling, I was able to explain. The words came easily and the whole time, he listened. But he wasn't simply listening. I knew that he understood.

We'd both been affected so dramatically. The entire episode was a crazy, mixed up, chaotic turn of events and the impact on both of us had been immense.

And when I later considered the coincidences that led to our chance meeting in the hallway, I wondered if it had all been part of a master plan; a predestined path that had been arranged to give us a chance to possibly reconnect once more. Even though I had hoped and prayed, it was something that I had not expected. Certainly not that day and not in that way.

And in addition, I definitely did not anticipate the scenario we found ourselves a part of next.

I also know for a fact that Ky certainly didn't expect it either.

Although I'm not sure who was more shocked. Him or me.

Caught out...

The whispered voices could easily be heard from behind the closed door. Although muffled, it was obvious that some sort of secretive conversation was underway. When a sudden giggle erupted however, Ky and I exchanged curious glances. It seemed that the storeroom was definitely occupied, but we had no idea by whom. Then, when the door swung abruptly open, I was sure that the surprised expressions on our own faces closely resembled the two that we were confronted with.

With a sideways glance at Ky, I raised my eyebrows in stunned silence, and then managed to mumble awkwardly, "Mrs. Greene asked us to drop these boxes off."

In an attempt to mask his surprise at the sight of two unexpected students staring questioningly back at him, Mr. Hathaway stammered, "Oh, that's fine. You can just put them inside."

Quickly managing to recover, he went on to explain, "I was just showing Sara the equipment we have available for the camp next week. If you can put the boxes down wherever you can find room, that'd be great."

Sara, who was standing silently beside the good looking Math teacher, had also managed to overcome her initial shocked reaction and pushed arrogantly past us. Then, with a slight flick of her blonde hair and a smug look in my direction, she was gone. Mr. Hathaway however, was forced to wait so that he could lock the door after we'd left.

Standing uncomfortably by, he appeared keen to share more

details, probably to add credibility to his story. "The school has purchased a heap of new gear. There's some new high tech compasses and some great camping equipment for the overnight campout. If you want me to run through what's available, let me know, because you're welcome to borrow anything you might need."

"Okay, thanks." Ky responded with a frown in his direction, before taking the last of the boxes from me and storing them in a corner.

Then, without another word from either of us, we quickly headed back in the direction from where we had come.

Not trusting myself to make a sound until I was sure we were out of earshot, I finally opened my mouth to speak, unable to keep my thoughts to myself any longer.

"OMG! That was so awkward!" Although my mind was racing, it was the only thing I could manage to say.

"Do I just have a vivid imagination?" Ky replied, shaking his head in disbelief. "Or was that what I think it was!"

Glancing around to make sure no one was nearby to hear our conversation and in particular, Mr. Hathaway himself, I lowered my voice just in case. "I know it looked suspicious, but there's a slight chance he was telling the truth."

Ky was staring at me, clearly dumbfounded at the scene we had just left behind. "Are you blind, Julia? Didn't you see their reaction! Obviously they were doing more than just checking equipment!"

"We don't know for sure, Ky! We don't really have any proof!" His response was causing me to panic, the acknowledgement of what we'd just witnessed too crazy to comprehend.

My gut instinct was complete paranoia at the thought of being involved in anything Sara was a part of. I just wanted to forget the whole incident had even happened.

"Julia, his body language said it all! And besides, why would the two of them be in there with the door shut? It's totally obvious."

Unable to argue, I sighed heavily before continuing. "I've had my suspicions for a while," I admitted reluctantly, "But I've never been completely sure."

"What? You already knew about this?" he shook his head, unable to fully understand the situation. "How long has it been going on?"

Nodding my head in resignation, I realized I had to tell him what I'd been keeping secret for so long. "A couple of months ago, Becky and I spotted Sara getting into Mr. Hathaway's car outside the shopping center. But I swore Becky to secrecy because I was worried about spreading rumors when we weren't certain of the facts. And then I caught them deep in conversation outside his classroom one afternoon, and it really didn't look as though they were discussing schoolwork. I haven't mentioned it to anyone else at all, not even Millie."

"You've got to admit it's pretty creepy!" The disgust on Ky's face showed exactly how he felt. "He's so much older than her. I can't believe she'd even want to be with him."

Ky continued on, his contempt for the situation making it easy for me to predict what was coming next.

"I think we should tell someone!"

I stared back at him and shook my head. "I don't know if that's a good idea, Ky. I really don't want to get involved!"

"He's a teacher, Julia. We can't let him get away with this. Plus, you've seen how skinny Sara is. It's not normal to look like that. She's probably got some sort of psychological disorder and he's taking full advantage of it."

Standing stock still, I took a moment to consider the repercussions of staying quiet. Perhaps keeping it a secret was the wrong thing to do. And the more I thought about it, the more I wondered whether he may actually be right.

Filled with increasing indecision, I knew it was a problem I could have done without. I certainly had enough to worry about without adding Sara to the mix. In the blink of an eye, my relief at the possibility of reconnecting with Ky had been completely shattered by something so bizarre and unexpected that it seemed almost surreal.

But then I came to my senses. Her confident stare as she'd sauntered past us, and the arrogant smug look she directed my way, had been enough to make my skin crawl. Deep down, I really was afraid of her. And although I hated to admit it, even to myself, the fear was real and there was nothing I could do about it.

So, without another moment's hesitation, I blurted, "You don't know her the way I do, Ky. You have no idea what she's capable of! She's seriously psycho. I've seen what she can do and I refuse to get involved. She's always hated me and there's no way I want to provoke her. Trust me. It's just not worth it."

Ky stared back dismayed and momentarily speechless at my abrupt response. Although I'd quite adamantly expressed my feelings about the situation, I could see that he was still unsure whether to agree.

Then, as the seconds ticked by, he finally nodded in consent. "Okay, Julia. If you feel that strongly about it, I won't say anything. Not for now, anyway. And hopefully after being caught out today, Mr. Hathaway will come to his senses. But I guess we'll just have to wait and see."

"Believe me," I tried to sound as convincing as possible, "Some things are better left alone and I really think this is one of them."

Interrupted by the sound of the bell signaling the end of lunch break, we headed silently towards our classrooms, each of us consumed by what had just taken place.

Even though we had no proof, we were both well aware that what we'd just witnessed was not simply an innocent meeting of a teacher and his student. That was a ridiculous explanation for finding the two of them in a remote storeroom on the far side of the school together. After what I'd seen in the past, it was just too coincidental. And I shook my head for the umpteenth time that day at the mystery of how various moments in life sometimes come to pass. The fact that we'd been asked to go to that exact location at the very time they happened to be there, was too strange to be accidental.

Perhaps we were meant to find them. Perhaps it was another predestined moment where we'd been given the chance to report something serious that really should not be allowed to continue.

But that girl scared me. She was mean and vindictive and as I had said to Ky, she was capable of anything. Regardless of the fact that the incident really should be reported, I didn't dare cross that line.

And besides, I had enough problems of my own right then, the least of which was worrying about Sara and her "friendship" with one of our school teachers. I was much more concerned about the boy walking alongside me.

We'd certainly been given the opportunity to clear the air between us and for that I was truly grateful. But would we ever return to the relationship we had shared so intensely such a short time ago?

Whether or not his memory would ever be fully restored, I had no idea. But as for his feelings towards me, I could only hope.

Was there a chance for us?

I guessed right then that only time would tell.

The bus trip...

When we were all seated on the bus ready to depart for Kappa Falls, the sight of Ky sitting across the aisle, filled me with nervous but hopeful anticipation. Eternally grateful for the fact that we'd been placed into the same group, I dared to dream that it was a sign we'd been given a second chance. A chance to spend time together and for Ky to get to know me again.

As I chatted excitedly to Millie, who was sitting alongside me, I was constantly aware of his presence nearby. One time, I caught him glancing in our direction and the shivers that tingled unexpectedly down my spine caused me to quickly catch my breath. My feelings for him were as intense as ever and I smiled anxiously to myself as I lay my head against the headrest, trying to calm my racing pulse.

There were so many students in our grade and the camp could not cater for us all at once. We'd been separated into two groups, and it was arranged so that while one group was at camp, the other remained at school. To our huge delight, we were in group one and the first to depart, whereas the second group were forced to wait until the following week.

The arrangement of the two groups however, had been organized by the teachers. Apparently their reasoning behind this was that they wanted us to mix with some people who weren't our closest friends. As it turned out, there were several kids on the bus who I barely recognized at all; people who, even though they were in my grade, I obviously hadn't ever really met.

Once again though, it seemed that destiny had played a part. Looking discreetly across the aisle in Ky's direction, I recalled the moment we were all informed of our groups. Millie and I had sat with fingers crossed and it was almost like winning a lottery prize when we found that we'd ended up together. And then to top it all off, I soon learned that Becky, Jess and Ky were also included. Of course hearing Ky's name had definitely caused the most excitement, and I'd barely been able to contain myself at the thought of a week away on camp with both Millie and Ky.

While this seemed to be the best scenario I could ever have hoped for, there was another that I was struggling to come to terms with and although I tried to brush the thought aside, it continued to haunt me.

The issue involved Sara Hamilton. She was also in group one. How was it that we kept being thrown together? I wanted nothing to do with her!

Ever since our accidental meeting outside the school store room a week earlier, I had done my best to avoid her. On the odd occasion where we'd crossed paths, her pointed look in my direction had carried a clear message; one that I did not need to have spelled out. In short, she was telling me to keep my mouth shut or else. And although that had been my intention anyway, she obviously did not feel secure enough to let it drop.

Unfortunately, she was the one person who had the potential to totally ruin my week. This was something I was well aware of but hoped would not be the case. Just the night before, memories of our Seventh Grade camp came flooding back; the nightmare of Sara leaving me locked in a deserted cabin, not only in the middle of dense bushland but also in the dead of night, too vivid and frightening a scene to ever forget. That memory stayed foremost in my mind while

I finished all the last minute packing until eventually I managed to force the vision away, determined to prevent her from spoiling my fun.

Interestingly enough though, I noticed that at the last minute Mr. Hathaway, who was one of the organizing teachers, had swapped places and was now accompanying the second group when they left the following week. At first I wondered what had caused the sudden change of plan but then intuition reminded me that our chance encounter the week before most probably had something to do with it. Perhaps he'd decided it would simply be too risky for himself and Sara to be on camp together and had taken it into his own hands to ensure that did not happen.

A few students had also arranged last minute swaps from one group to another, although I had no idea how they'd managed to get permission. Knowing that Sara was capable of anything, it seemed curious that she had not arranged a swap for herself. And I wondered how she'd responded to the news that she and Mr. Hathaway would not be going on camp together.

But then, deciding to forget about Sara for the time being, I tuned into the animated conversation going on around me. While everyone was clearly enthusiastic about the prospect of a week away from school, several still had quite serious reservations about what lay ahead and some had previously needed convincing from their teachers and friends, before agreeing to take part. The cause of their apprehension was due to the style of camp and the activities that were in store for us, some of which were very different to anything we had ever experienced before.

During our stay, we all had to spend one night camping out alone, unaccompanied by an adult or a friend or anyone else for that matter. And in addition, our individual camp sites were pre-allocated by one of the camp instructors and would not be placed in the vicinity of anyone else. During that night, we were given the task to erect our own tent and fend for ourselves. This included organizing our own pre-prepared meals which would probably consist of some fruit and something from a can or packet. The reason for this was because fires were not allowed due to the danger involved.

As if that experience in itself was not enough of a challenge, they had thrown one other monumental scenario into the mix. All forms of technology were banned. This meant no mobile phones, no iPads, computers, iPods or any type of electronic device whatsoever was allowed to be brought along. And that was the absolute killer rule for everyone. Surviving an entire week without a mobile phone and having no access to social media was probably going to be the hardest challenge of all.

The idea of a night alone in the bush, with no friends as well as no technology, was a daunting one. And we were all pretty apprehensive about it.

"What will we do all night?" one of the boys at school had asked a teacher.

"You could try reading a book!" had been the teacher's quick response, and the boy had rolled his eyes.

It was something that had clearly not occurred to him and it obviously didn't interest him either.

As I actually enjoyed reading, this was something I looked forward to and had made sure I packed plenty of books to keep me going during our stay. However, while I quite looked forward to a night of camping, I did feel slightly concerned about the thought of a night camping alone in the dark.

Although most of us felt the same way about this particular activity, the overall excitement was too great to let it dampen our spirits. And Millie and I chatted non-stop, all the while raising our voices in an effort to be heard over the laughter and loud noise from the students surrounding us.

After we'd been driving for a while and the atmosphere had quietened down somewhat, I had a sudden urge to turn around and glance down the aisle, curious to see what everyone at the rear of the bus was up to. While scanning the scene behind me, my eyes fell upon a person who I hadn't given very much thought to over the past weeks. Although I'd seen him around school and we did share the same English class, we rarely spoke or had anything to do with each other. I'd certainly had way too much on my mind of late, to be noticing what Blake Jansen was up to.

Just at that very moment…the two of us happened to make eye contact and instantly the familiar and heart-warming smile that I remembered so well, appeared on his face as soon as he saw me glancing in his direction.

A lively tingle crept over my skin and I smiled awkwardly in return, my own reaction completely unexpected. I found it hard to believe that he still had the power to affect me in that way. The fact that we were both included in the same camp group was also another interesting coincidence that had taken place.

However, as I turned back towards the front, I spotted Ky deep in conversation with the person next to him and for the time being, all thoughts of Blake Jansen left my mind.

That was until a short time later when I overheard some interesting gossip.

Blake and his girlfriend, Monica were no longer together. She had dumped him for a senior guy at our school. No-one seemed aware of the details, except for the fact that she'd been one of the students to swap from our group to the other one. This explained her absence on our bus.

Fate was such a weird thing sometimes. I wondered momentarily about the fact that Blake was single once again, all the while not wanting to admit to myself that I did find that scenario an interesting one.

But then, realizing we'd finally arrived at our destination, I stood abruptly, keen to be amongst the first to get off the bus, all other thoughts disappearing completely.

Arrival...

My first impression of Kappa Falls was even better than I'd expected. We had all previously been told various stories by seniors who had already taken part in the camp and we knew fairly well what was ahead for us. But the moment I hopped off the bus, my level of excitement increased even more.

The view across the valley from where we stood was amazing and we could see nearby groups of cabins and other buildings scattered amongst clusters of leafy green trees. We could also see a winding river situated at the bottom of the hill and on its banks were a variety of canoes and other equipment, ready for use in the water. It was perfect that the weather had turned warm because we'd heard so much about the cool rope swing that was attached to a branch of a tree and we couldn't wait to try it out.

As well as all the fun that I knew was in store, I particularly looked forward to the idea of spending the next seven days in a country setting. It reminded me of the property where we'd lived before moving back to Carindale. And an instant flashback to that wonderful period in my life flooded quickly to mind.

However, I had little time to daydream because it was first in, first served for the cabin beds, and after collecting our belongings, I raced the other girls to the cabin that we'd been allocated. Thankfully we had been allowed to organize our own cabin groups and Millie, Becky, Jess and I had formed a group with other friends of Millie's, each of us, keen to unpack and settle in.

Our cabin had two bunk rooms with four beds in each and a central living area. There was a table, four chairs and a couple of couches. These items, along with the bunk beds in the bedrooms, were the extent of the furniture.

When everyone had claimed a bed and started to unpack, it seemed that within minutes, the entire floor of our room was covered mainly in Becky's belongings. She had brought so many clothes, there appeared to be an almost endless supply. What caught my attention, was not so much the amount of clothing but the contents of a large plastic bag which had spilled out onto the timber flooring. Numerous packets of crisps, sweets, popcorn and gum lay there, waiting to be eaten!

While we'd all been pre-warned that junk food was to be limited, this certainly hadn't stopped Becky. Most people had bags of treats hidden in their bags but after looking through the selection on our bedroom floor right then, it was clear that Becky would most likely win the prize for the largest supply.

"What?" she said, in response to the astonished looks she was getting from Millie and myself. "You can't expect me to survive an entire week on camp food? These are emergency supplies. And I bet you'll be glad that I brought them!"

With a burst of laughter, Millie quickly advised her to keep her large stash hidden away, warning her that if our teachers found it, they'd probably confiscate at least half. And so Becky, with a frustrated shake of her head, gathered the items together and shoved them all back into her oversized suitcase.

Although I found Becky's abundance of treats quite amusing, I was grateful for the fact that she hadn't brought any alcohol. This was also the scenario with everyone else in our cabin. A few people in other cabin groups had smuggled in a supply by camouflaging it in water bottles.

For us, the strict warning from our teachers that any culprits would be made to leave camp, was enough to stop us from even considering the idea. The clincher was probably the fact that parents would be called to collect anyone caught drinking, which would be a pretty embarrassing situation to be a part of.

This was something that had actually happened to a couple of boys the previous year and I was surprised that anyone would risk bringing alcohol this time. Especially as the teachers had stressed that if it occurred again, there would also be the threat of suspension from school.

I had no idea who amongst our grade might be involved or whether it was simply a rumor, but right then, I didn't really care. All I was concerned about was getting my things unpacked and finding a place in the cupboard to put them before Becky shoved all her belongings in.

Before long though, we were all pretty well organized and as we still had half an hour or so before morning tea, decided to check out some of the other cabins. With Ky constantly in my thoughts, I wondered briefly where his cabin was situated. While most of the boys had been placed on the other side of the property, a couple of the groups had been given cabins nearby and I secretly hoped that Ky's might be one of them.

When Millie spotted one of her friends on the veranda of the cabin next to ours, I decided to follow her lead and headed up the steps behind her, with Becky and Jess also in tow. But as soon as I walked through the door, I instantly wished that I hadn't.

Standing awkwardly by as Millie chatted on in her usual

friendly manner, all I could manage to do was fake a small smile and pretend that I hadn't noticed Sara's seething glare; one that was clearly intended to make me feel very unwelcome.

I hadn't realized that she was included in that group and would definitely not have joined Millie if I'd known. But it seemed that no one else was aware of the tension, so I attempted to ignore her and join in the conversation around me.

However, Sara was not satisfied with that and clearly not at all happy to have me standing there invading her space. Obviously unable to keep her mouth shut where I was concerned, she drew all attention my way by loudly blurting out a snide remark; one that was totally unanticipated and very, very cruel.

"So, Julia, how's things with Ky? Has his memory returned yet? It must be so hard for you, you poor thing!"

Knowing full well that she was aware of the details of his accident and also that there was not one genuine ounce of sympathy whatsoever in her comment, I looked furiously back at her, unable to hide my contempt.

Thankfully though, Millie, who could see my instant distress, managed to murmur something in response, and then tactfully went on to change the subject in an attempt to direct all attention away from me. But this did not distract Sara who continued to stare scornfully in my direction.

Seething quietly inside, I could not stand to be near her a moment longer and excused myself pretending that I'd left something behind in my room.

Then, as I headed quickly down the steps and onto the pavement, eager to be as far away from her as possible, I bumped unexpectedly into a group of boys heading towards the hall.

And in the middle of them all, looking curiously towards me, was Ky.

Confrontation…

With my face flushed and tears threatening at the corners of my eyes, the sight of the boys blocking my path, simply added to my discomfort, and I quickly attempted to hide my misery.

"Hey," I stammered, "How's everything going?"

"Great," Ky replied. "Seems like a pretty cool place!"

"Yeah, it looks awesome." I tried to sound enthusiastic as my eyes darted towards his group of friends, but I just looked more awkward than ever.

Feeling an embarrassed flush creep over my skin, I stood there uncomfortably, completely at a loss for what to say next. It was definitely one of those moments that one later regrets and I cursed myself for being so uptight and making such a fool of myself.

Wanting to escape the odd looks from the boys, Ky included, I abruptly moved off, after saying that I would see them in the hall. Aware of their curious stares as I headed past, I put my head down and kept walking.

"OMG!" I muttered to myself as I pushed open the cabin door and made my way into the bathroom, closing the door shut behind me. "You're such a loser, Julia!"

Hissing the words in frustration, I stared at my reflection in the mirror before bending over to splash cool water onto my face and neck; anything to avoid looking at myself right then.

"How can you let her affect you like that?"

Shaking my head with self-loathing I splashed more water onto my skin, unable to come to terms with my embarrassing behavior. I could not believe that I had allowed Sara to bring me to tears and then, to make matters even worse, that I would totally embarrass myself in front of Ky and his friends.

It was all so pathetic, and I knew that I really had to get myself together or the camp would be a disaster.

Looking into the mirror once more, I took a deep breath, and stared at the face of the girl in front of me.

"This is ridiculous! You have to stop letting her push you around!"

Speaking the words out loud seemed to strengthen my resolve and a look of steely determination crept slowly over my features.

Knowing that a couple of the other girls were still in the cabin, and would probably be wondering why I remained locked in the bathroom, I forced myself to take another deep breath and open the door. Everyone, it appeared, was heading to the hall and I did not want to be left behind.

I knew that I all I had to do was stand up to Sara. She had previously ruined one camp and it was up to me to make sure that she didn't ruin another. Aware that if I allowed her to think she had the upper hand, she would simply continue to make my life hell, I realized that I just had to stop letting her get to me.

Determined to stay strong, I made my way with the others along the pathway to join Millie, Becky and Jess. But as soon as I fell into step alongside Millie, she gave me a concerned glance.

"Are you okay?" she whispered quietly, not wanting to draw attention from the others.

"Yeah, I'm fine!" I replied, forcing a quick grin. "Just looking forward to some food. I'm starving!"

Then, chatting randomly about anything I could think of, I continued along beside her, preferring to avoid talking about Sara. In particular, I really did not want to admit that the girl who had caused me so much misery throughout middle school was still a major problem in my life. It was something that I wanted to deal with on my own. And besides, dwelling on the Sara issue made me angrier than ever. I just wanted to stay out of her way altogether.

However, on entry to the dining area, all thoughts of Sara were quickly replaced with pangs of hunger as I found myself faced with a long trestle type table covered with delicious looking food. As well as chocolate muffins, which are my all-time favorite, there was also a variety of other flavored muffins and several large platters of fruit. It was obvious that there would be no shortage of food while we were on camp and I eagerly joined the long queue waiting in line to help themselves to the selection.

When I finally reached the front of the line, there was only one chocolate muffin left and I quickly leaned over to add it to the small plate of fruit that I already had in my hand. Feeling grateful that I'd managed to grab the last one, I turned to join my friends who were rushing to claim one of the few available tables positioned on the outside veranda. The view of the valley from that spot was beautiful and a perfect place to sit while we ate.

In my haste however, I happened to accidentally brush past a group of girls who were also making their way outside.

Looking up to apologize, I found myself staring into the face of the one person I'd promised myself I would either avoid or stand up to. But the look of outrage on her face, instantly melted away any courage on my part and I stood stock still in front of her.

"Seriously, can't you watch where you're going?"

Sara's loud, sarcastic comment drew the attention of everyone nearby and I felt my face redden for the second time that morning. It was obviously a gross over reaction on her part but where I was concerned, she never seemed to hold back. It was what she did next though, that really made my blood boil.

Pushing roughly past me and intentionally shoving into my shoulder, she caused the cup of juice that I was holding, to spill. All I could do was jump back in reaction to the cold sensation soaking through the light fabric of my t-shirt onto my skin underneath. Looking down at the orange stain covering the entire front of my top, I realized that the spilled juice had also drowned everything on my plate.

Frustrated and angry, I made my way to the nearest rubbish bin and dumped the spoiled plate of food. My appetite had abruptly disappeared, but not wanting to let her get the best of me, I quickly grabbed an apple and another cup of juice, before heading outside to join my friends.

When I walked past her table, I immediately felt my skin crawl and as I glanced reluctantly towards her, her cold arrogant smirk at the sight of my stained t-shirt, caused a chill to work its way down my spine. Angry with my ridiculous reaction, I forced myself to maintain eye contact and glare defiantly back.

But by the time I reached my group of friends, who sat waiting for me to join them, a sick and nauseous sensation had taken hold. Taking a deep breath, I convinced myself to remain calm. And, unable to resist the temptation, I looked briefly towards her once again.

I had not expected to find her still staring at me however, and was tempted to look quickly away. But, an inner strength I didn't know existed came quickly to the fore. Rather than allowing her to overpower me as was usually the case, I managed to stare back, a determined expression clear on my face.

When I noticed the glint of surprise that registered in her features, I felt my mouth curve slightly into a mildly confident grin. Then turning back towards Millie and the others, I proceeded to join in their conversation, the unease in my stomach disappearing momentarily at least. It was only a very small, very minor victory but definitely a satisfying one and I bit hungrily into my apple.

Feeling quite sure that it was going to be an interesting week, I reminded myself that it was up to me to make it a good one.

And this time, Sara was not going to win.

Just Friends...

Our first morning at camp involved several group activities. To begin with, there were some leadership and confidence building games and activities where we had to mix with boys and girls from different cabins. But much to my disappointment, I found that Millie, Becky, Jess and I had all been separated. To make matters worse, Ky had also been placed into another group.

Pre-arranged by our teachers, my entire group, it seemed, was made up of people who were not my close friends. When the instructor directed everyone to find a partner, I was left standing alone and feeling slightly uncomfortable, because apart from me, everyone else had managed to form a pair.

Just as I was preparing myself for the idea of having to partner with the instructor, a couple of boys who were running late appeared from nowhere and I found myself being asked to join them to form a group of three. Feeling very apprehensive, I moved to a spot alongside Blake, finding it hard to believe that out of everyone on camp, I had been placed with him and his friend. Then, standing awkwardly alongside them, I forced myself to listen to the instructions. However, I certainly did not expect what was in store.

The task we were being instructed to complete involved being blindfolded and then led through bushland to a spot a few hundred meters away. This required trust in your partner and while there was a lot of giggling and laughing from other pairs, when Blake rushed to be the first to lead me along the track, the awkwardness of the situation became more intense than ever.

It would have been bad enough to have some random boy who I barely knew lead me through the bush, but having Blake's hand in mine, brought back too many memories.

The chance that I should be paired with him seemed too bizarre to be real and that very thought was what raced through my mind as I felt his hand grip a firm hold of my own. Thankfully though, having his friend, Jack there to accompany us along the way seemed to ease the tension a little. Jack was outgoing and very funny and before long, all three of us were cracking up at his comments and humor, along with his efforts to scare me with unknown obstacles that didn't really exist.

When we finally reached our destination and had to swap places, Blake and I were left on our own while Jack was asked to partner someone else. And it was with a pleased grin that Blake reached out for my hand after tying the blindfold securely at the back of his head.

Feeling more relaxed because I was in control this time, I could not help the smile that had formed on my own face. Reluctant to admit that I was actually enjoying his attention, I continued to lead him through the bush…laughing and joking at the sight of him staggering along. At one stage, he tripped on a tree root and almost fell on top of me, I wondered whether it had been intentional. With his hands clutching my shoulders in an attempt to regain his balance, the grin that remained glued to his features did not betray any signs of concern. Then when the same thing happened a few meters further down the track, I was convinced that it was definitely not accidental.

Throughout the rest of the session, I could feel his gaze constantly being directed my way and at one point, we made eye contact from across the circle where we were sitting. Quickly glancing away, I tried to stifle the smile that threatened at the corners of my mouth and I forced myself to continue looking elsewhere.

Making our way back towards the cabins at the end of the session, he fell into step alongside me, and it was instantly obvious that the old easy-going familiarity between us had returned. I realized how much I'd missed his company but at the same time, was surprised at the happy and excited feeling that had taken hold.

Confused by the sudden change in my feelings towards him, I entered my cabin and sat down to wait for my girlfriends to arrive so we could all go to lunch together. Then a subconscious reminder, Ky's face, flashed quickly into view.

Unsure of how I felt right then, I focused on the afternoon session which involved canoeing and swimming in the river. That was the one activity that everyone was looking forward to.

I was aware that my own excitement towards what lay ahead had definitely increased somewhat but I was also aware of why. Preferring to ignore my confused state of mind however, I decided to simply enjoy the moment as well as the attention I was receiving.

It was all innocent fun. Blake and I were just friends and what could possibly be the harm in that?

What's going on?...

The rope swing out onto the water turned out to be the coolest thing ever. Although the river was freezing, the air temperature was very warm and many of us were keen to swim. We were able to use the canoes as well and this proved to be heaps of fun, especially as everyone was attempting to capsize the other boats. This resulted in everyone swimming whether they had intended to or not. Overall though, what everyone enjoyed the most was definitely the swing and girls' screams could constantly be heard as they let go and tumbled into the water.

Amongst the chaos and laughter, something I noticed was that although Sara's cabin group were amongst the rest of us, Sara was nowhere to be seen. While I was completely grateful for her absence, I was curious as to why she wasn't there. But after giving the situation more thought, I realized that it wasn't such a surprise after all and wondered if she ever would join in any activities that involved swimming.

Most of the girls were wearing bikinis and I wondered what Sara would look like.

It was hard to forget how amazing her body had looked in the past and I had often envied her beautiful figure. Nowadays however, her body shape was completely different and I was still unable to understand how she could be happy with the way she looked. Regardless of her tiny frame, she did appear to eat fairly generous portions of food at morning tea and lunch. So I guessed she must be continuing to throw up her meals after eating. It was a gross thought but there could be no other explanation.

I had no idea how she would manage to hide such a condition while on camp; especially while staying in a cabin and forced to share the bathroom. Although, knowing how sneaky Sara could be, I was sure that she had become quite skilled at keeping her behavior secret when necessary.

What amazed me was Mr. Hathaway's interest in a girl who was so thin and I wondered how he or anyone else could find her attractive. Her body looked like a skeleton! But then I was reminded of her beautiful face and flowing tresses of gorgeous blonde hair. And although her body shape was tiny she was still pretty big up top. I just couldn't understand how on earth it was fair to be so skinny and still manage to be attractive. Added to that was her outgoing personality and flirty manner, so I guessed that all of this combined was a huge attraction for guys, regardless of their age group.

As for what went on inside her head, I had no idea, except for the fact that she clearly resented me. But when thoughts came to mind of her anorexia or bulimia (I still wasn't sure what the correct term for her particular condition was), it gave me a deeper understanding of her pent up anger. It still didn't explain the reason I remained her prime target though and I just wished she would find someone else to pick on.

Standing on the bank deep in thought, I was completely unprepared for the sudden shove that came from behind. And when I was unexpectedly thrust into the river, I squealed loudly in response.

Pushing my way through the water, I finally broke the surface and gulped down a breath of much needed air, while at the same time looking towards the bank where I'd been standing, in search of the culprit. Expecting to see Millie, Becky or perhaps even Ky watching me and laughing hysterically, I was surprised that none of my close friends were in view at all. In fact, there was no one in that general area who seemed to be remotely interested or aware that I'd just been pushed in.

My attention was then redirected by a huge splash from behind and I turned around to find Blake grinning with obvious amusement. Laughing in surprise, I splashed him back and a friendly banter erupted between us, with him chasing after me in an attempt to dunk my head beneath the water.

Swimming towards a nearby canoe in order to grab hold of the edge so I could catch my breath, I looked behind once more, expecting to find him in hot pursuit. But he was nowhere to be seen. As I scanned the area however, what did catch my attention was the sight of Ky sitting alongside Millie and a couple of other girls on the riverbank, chatting animatedly and clearly enjoying himself. I knew that they had all been placed into the same group earlier that morning and when I later asked Millie who she was paired up with, she had replied briefly that it was one of the boys, and then changed the subject completely.

At the time I hadn't thought too much of it but from my spot in the water, I could see that she and Ky were getting on very well, and I took a sudden interest in the scene in front of me.

The fact that the two people I treasured most had become good friends was something I was aware I should be thankful for. I had previously hoped that they would get on well and that it would also help to bring Ky and myself closer together. But right then, for some reason, I felt a sudden urgency to join them.

With all thoughts of Blake disappearing, I began to swim towards the shore. It was a chance for me to hang out with

Ky and this was something I hadn't yet had the opportunity to do. But as I made my way through the water, my view was interrupted by a couple of canoes that were being paddled past and I was forced to wait before I could continue. When they finally moved out of the way and I once more had a clear view of the bank, I could not see Millie or Ky or any of the others in their group anywhere.

As soon as I reached the edge, I spotted Becky and Jess who were waving for me to join them. They were sitting with a few others in the shade of a nearby tree so I grabbed my towel and headed in their direction.

"Have you seen Millie?" I asked curiously, as I sat down alongside Becky. "She was just over there a few minutes ago but now I can't see her anywhere."

Without a word, Becky indicated with a nod of her head towards the hill behind us and following her gaze, I noticed a group making their way up the steep incline. Instantly, I recognized Millie's hot pink towel, which was tied securely around her waist. I had been admiring it earlier that afternoon and as I watched her climb the steep slope, it stood out brightly against the green backdrop of the grassy hill.

The fact that she had left without me was somewhat unexpected but what I found even more surprising was the sight of the boy deep in conversation alongside her. Even though they were quite a distance away, I could tell that it was Ky. I knew that I would recognize him anywhere.

When I caught Becky's expression and the way she raised her eyebrows in response to the scene in front of us, I could see that she was also curious as to the friendship that had appeared to have developed so rapidly.

"They've probably just had enough of the water." I was

aware that my words were a pretty lame excuse but I needed to justify their actions, for my own piece of mind at least.

"Yeah, probably," she replied and without another word on the topic, turned back towards Jess and the conversation going on around us.

Although she had not said much, her expression and the sarcasm in her voice spoke volumes. But knowing that it wasn't like Becky to stir up trouble, I forced myself to believe that she had completely misinterpreted the situation.

Regardless of my efforts though, I was finding it very difficult to overcome the sinking sensation that had begun to form in the pit of my stomach.

The gathering…

That evening after dinner everyone sat in small groups around a huge bonfire that had been set up in the middle of a clearing, a short distance away from the cabins. Although there were strict camp rules that we'd all been made aware of, we were given a free reign during times that didn't require us to participate in organized activities. The bonfire was one of those occasions where we could take part if we chose.

Because the camp was so isolated, there weren't too many alternatives so I guessed that made it easy to give us a fair amount of freedom. And there wasn't too much mischief anyone could get up to, or so the organizers probably thought.

Being the first night however, a few people decided they wanted to make the most of it and went to lengths to put some other plans into place. Becky, Jess and I only heard about this because Millie had been invited to join in and she was keen for us to also tag along.

"You guys should come too! We're just going to hang out in one of the cabins. It'll be fun!" she promised, as she looked at each of us in turn.

As usual, her convincing and excitable manner made the offer too hard to refuse and besides, it definitely sounded more fun than spending the next couple of hours sitting around a bonfire.

Becky loved being friends with Millie. Although I think her real motivation was because Millie was friends with all the cool people in our grade. Her outgoing personality made her popular with everyone, so she found it really easy to fit in.

At first I was hesitant in case Sara was involved but after some slight hesitation, decided I didn't want to be left behind. The other girls were keen, so I did not want to allow Sara to spoil my fun. In addition, my small stand-off at morning tea that morning had given me some much needed confidence and I was actually looking forward to confronting her again.

However, it seemed to take Becky forever to decide on an outfit to wear and after several changes of clothes, Millie became so impatient, she threatened to go without us. Then, because we were in such a rush to leave the cabin, no one apart from Millie thought to bring a flashlight and this made it difficult to see the darkened track that we were forced to follow.

In an effort to avoid drawing attention to ourselves, we had chosen to stay away from the main pathway. Although a gathering of a few people seemed innocent enough, our gut instincts told us that our teachers probably wouldn't approve. Plus it was invitation only, and we certainly didn't want a heap of other people asking to join us.

I was aware of my doubts about what was in store but too caught up in the excitement from the other girls, I chose to ignore any concerns that had surfaced.

What was still playing on my mind though, was Millie's sudden disappearance from the river earlier that afternoon. When I questioned her about it afterwards, she said that she hadn't been feeling well and wanted to return to the cabin for a rest. Then, at the sound of Ky's name, I was sure I noticed an odd reaction on her part as she appeared to falter for a moment before switching topics completely. It was almost as though she felt uncomfortable talking about him.

Rather than focusing on something that I hoped was purely

a figment of my imagination however, I concentrated on the pathway and finally we found the cabin we were looking for.

Much to our surprise, the place was in darkness, with all the lights turned off and no one in sight.

"Where is everyone?" Millie asked, the irritation evident in her voice. "I knew we should hurry. They've probably gone off somewhere else but who knows where!"

She was clearly not impressed to have missed the opportunity for some fun and I could see the annoyed expression on her face as she glared angrily at Becky. Surprised at her reaction, I opened my mouth to suggest that we take a look around, when we heard someone calling her name.

"Millie! We're down this way."

Turning towards the direction of the voice, we spotted a track leading down an embankment that led to a darkened area below. But with only the light of a single torch it was difficult to find our footing and I regretted for the second time, not bringing my own flashlight.

After some slipping and sliding and the odd squeal that was quickly hushed by the group at the bottom of the hill, we eventually managed to reach the level patch of ground where everyone was sitting.

"Keep your voices down, girls!" laughed a familiar voice. "We've found the perfect hiding spot and we don't want anyone to know we're here!"

Peering into the darkness, the glow of Millie's flashlight shone on Ky's face and I was taken aback for a moment at the sight of him standing in front of me. I certainly had not been prepared for this and I wondered briefly if Millie had been expecting to see him there.

My surprise at the fact that Ky and his friends were part of the group Millie had been invited to join, was overtaken by the next response. Although, if I was being honest with myself, I had to admit that I'd been expecting it.

"Do you girls want a drink? We have plenty!"

Looking around in the dim glow, I counted a group of 5 boys and 4 girls, but Sara was not amongst them. Instantly I knew this was something to be grateful for. I really didn't think I could cope with having her there right then as I soon found that I had plenty of other issues to contend with.

For me, the fear of being caught drinking alcohol while on camp was too great but it didn't seem to bother the others as they drank from the bottle that was being passed around. And with Millie sitting alongside Ky on the opposite side of the circle, all I could do was look on in frustrated silence. Before too long, the pair were chatting and laughing, although I had no idea what was so amusing. Obviously the alcohol was quickly taking effect but watching the two of them together made me more uncomfortable than ever.

It was so dark that we could barely see each other's faces. At one point, a flashlight shined on Millie and I caught a quick glance from her...I could not help but stare coldly back.

I tried to join in the laughter going on around me but was unable to control the despair I was feeling. By that stage, I desperately wanted to escape and was tempted to make the trip back to our cabin on my own. I just wanted to get away, but too scared to attempt the track by myself, especially without a flashlight, I was forced to suffer in silence.

That was until the laughter and loud voices surrounding me

were abruptly interrupted by the sound of an adult, calling down from the top of the hill.

"What's going on down there?"

As if in answer to the thoughts in my head, everyone instantly jumped to their feet, each of us forced to make a move whether we wanted to or not.

The unexpected shout had us scattering frantically in all directions. But although every flashlight had been switched off, the majority of the group had no control over their own voices and the sounds of stifled giggling seemed louder than ever.

Grabbing hold of Becky's arm, I dragged her along behind me, desperate to escape the beam from the high-powered torch that was shining in our direction. My fear of being spotted, was so great that I could feel my heart pounding wildly in my chest as I ran.

Stumbling through the long grass, I headed towards the dark outline of nearby trees, hoping to hide amongst them. At the same time however, the torch beam seemed to follow my every move.

With adrenalin kicking in, my feet sped over the rocky terrain as I dragged Becky into the thicket of bush. My wildly racing pulse felt ready to explode and I barely noticed the scratch of branches that scraped roughly against my skin.

My only concern right then was to stay hidden until we could attempt to make our way back to our cabin.

Just as we thought it was safe to make a move however, we were blinded by the bright light that shone directly into our faces.

Consequences...

When I saw Becky's dad pull up in his car late the following morning, the frown of serious disapproval was almost too much to bear. Glaring at Becky who was standing alongside me, he opened the car door and without a word, made his way over to our supervising teacher who had been waiting nearby for his arrival.

The whole scenario was more humiliating than I could ever have imagined and I could not believe that it had come about. My only saving grace was that my own dad was away for the week and unable to come and get me. To see his daughter evicted from her school camp would have filled him with shame and for me, his look of disappointment would have been worse than the punishment itself.

Climbing into the back of the car, I sat alongside Becky and stared out the window. In the distance, I could see groups of kids tackling a high ropes course that was set up in a cleared area at the bottom of the hill. From our vantage point in the car park, we had an open view and I realized abruptly, that the area I was staring at was actually right by the spot where we'd met for our gathering the night before.

It was also right by the trees where we'd attempted to hide.

Shaking my head in disbelief at what had taken place, I recalled the terrifying moment when the high-powered beam of the teacher's flashlight had found its mark. That exact moment, I was sure, would be etched on my mind forever. The mere recollection was frightening and my pulse began to race at the sound of his booming voice as it replayed continually in my mind.

"What do you two girls think you're doing?"

The fact that we'd been caught hiding out in the bush was bad enough but this was instantly worsened when the powerful beam of light fell upon the item that Becky still held in her hand. I simply couldn't understand why she hadn't dumped it somewhere in the bush! To stand there in full view with a half empty bottle of alcohol firmly in her grasp was beyond stupidity.

"I was too scared to move!" she moaned later that night after we'd been marched back to our cabin. "I was so scared that I completely forgot I was still holding it!"

Her attempt to explain fell on deaf ears as she apologized over and over.

In reality though, I knew it wasn't her fault and I really had no one but myself to blame.

"If only I hadn't gone with them in the first place!" I could not let the thought go and as I sat humiliated and ashamed, in the back seat of Becky's car, that single thought replayed over and over again in my mind.

For us, the worst part was that no one else had been caught. Somehow they had all managed to escape back to the safety of their cabins and Becky and I were left to face the aftermath.

The teachers had their suspicions of course, but when we were questioned, neither of us were willing to snitch on the others. I spoke up first, pretending ignorance, and said that we'd heard about a gathering but when we joined the group, it was too dark to see who was actually there. I also said that by then, most people had left anyway. I couldn't bring myself to start listing names, it just didn't seem the right thing to do. And I knew beyond doubt that if the situation were reversed, I'd be praying that the ones who were caught, would stay quiet and allow me to remain safe.

Staring pointedly at Becky as she shared her version of the events, I was relieved to find that she was willing to go along with my story. We'd been warned in simple terms that we should confess the truth or be forced to take the blame on our own. But as soon as I realized that we'd all share the same fate regardless, I decided there was no point involving the others.

For me, the most frustrating detail was the fact that I had been the only one not drinking alcohol. This was something that I decided the teachers should know about, but when I tried to convince them of the truth, they simply brushed it aside. According to them, I was still breaking the rules.

I really didn't think they believed me anyway and I could see that my innocence in that department was not going to help, whether they believed me or not. It was obvious they needed someone to punish and we were the scapegoats.

It was so unfair! I could not believe it!

I'd hardly slept the night before, and had spent the majority of the night, curled up wide awake in bed. Millie and Jess had been ready to admit to their involvement, but I persuaded them not to. Although it had taken some time to convince them both that there really was no point.

My main concern however, was the threat of suspension. The teachers hadn't said the Suspension word to Becky or myself. And I desperately hoped we could avoid such a dire consequence.

Tears of shame began to form at the corners of my eyes. But then I brushed them angrily away. The situation was bad enough and I did not want to make more of a scene than necessary. Especially as a group of kids were standing by and watching the spectacle take place.

Unfortunately for us, it seemed that morning tea was about to be served so there were several people milling around the dining hall which was situated right beside the car park.

I just wished that Becky's dad would hurry so we could get out of there. All I wanted to do was leave as quickly as possible.

Then when he finally climbed into the car and started the ignition, I caught sight of a group returning from their morning activity. It seemed at that moment, my worst fears were coming to fruition. Millie and Ky were walking alongside each other, and from my spot in the car, I could clearly see the animated smile on Ky's face as he looked towards her.

That simple smile was what hurt more than anything. Never before had I anticipated the scene before me. And while it could all be seen as an innocent friendship, intuition told me differently.

With a misty veil of tears beginning to cloud my view, I turned away, not wanting to look at the pair any longer. But out of the corner of my eye, I spotted a flicker of movement and was forced to turn around once more.

Staring through the rear window, I looked curiously on, while the tall, muscular figure ran in our direction; as if to catch up with the departing car, making its way slowly down the gravel driveway.

And then, in an instant, the cloud of tears cleared and recognition dawned. Blake's familiar stance had not changed. But what stood out most, was the distraught look on his face as he watched us disappear down the road. Even from that distance, I could see that his sympathy was genuine, and for that I was truly grateful.

My eyes remained on his until eventually we were too far away and he was out of sight. Then I turned to face the front, the shock of the previous 12 hours filling me with a numb silence.

***

Find out what happens next in...

Julia Jones – The Teenage Years

Book 5

Coming Soon!

Thank you for reading

Book 4

'MAYHEM'

If you enjoyed it, could I please ask you to leave a review?

Thank you so much!

Katrina x

Follow Julia Jones on Instagram @juliajonesdiary

and

Please Like our Facebook page

to keep updated on the release date for each new book in the series...

www.facebook.com/JuliaJonesDiary

ANNOUNCING A NEW SERIES!!

This fabulous new series fills the gap after Julia was forced to move to the country with her family.

It continues the story of Julia Jones' Diary but has a whole new twist, one that all Julia Jones' Diary fans are sure to enjoy.

A new girl called Emmie unexpectedly arrives in Carindale and meets Millie. But Emmie has a secret, a secret that must remain hidden at all costs.

What happens to Julia, Blake, Sara and all the others and how does Emmie's sudden appearance impact Julia and her friends?

Find out now in

<u>Mind Reader – Book 1: My New Life</u>

OUT NOW!!

Be sure to check out the exciting and suspenseful series…

Angel

Book 1

Guardian

18523099R00069

Printed in Great Britain
by Amazon